Your Hand in Mine

LILY FOSTER

SHOREFRONT BOOKS

Also by Lily Foster

THE LET ME SERIES

Let Me Be the One

Let Me Love You

Let Me Go

Let Me Heal Your Heart

Let Me Fall

When I Let You Go

THE BLACKBIRD SERIES

When the Night is Over

Your Hand in Mine

Ghost on the Shore

All Your Life

First paperback edition October 2020

IBSN 9780998916743 (ebook)
IBSN 9780998916750 (paperback)

Cover: Megan Barker Designs

Your Hand in Mine

Part One

THE LONG GOODBYE

<h1 style="text-align:center"></h1>

SKYLAR

No one says it.

They shake their heads, dab a tissue to the corner of one eye, say things like: *Such a good man, Such a lovely couple, So devoted to one another and to their two beautiful girls.*

It's obvious what's on the mind of every single person crammed around the dining room table, but no one asks: *What do you think* really *happened that night? I didn't know they were having problems, did you? How will the girls manage without them?*

Nope. They lay their contributions to the sob fest down on the table, a gooey casserole or some sticky-sweet cake, then go on eulogizing my father like he's some modern-day Ward Cleaver.

Who made the tuna noodle casserole? That's what I want to know. It wasn't Sienna, that's for sure. She would have fashioned parsley leaves or carrot sticks into the shape of a fish to decorate the top.

My twin sister did make the strawberry shortcake, though. I'm sure of it. The blueberries clustered in one corner along with the rows of uniformly cut strawberries make the cake into an adorable replica of the American flag. My heart aches at the sight of it. Always looking to please, always making lemonade when life kicks you in the ass and gives you lemons. Decorating a damn cake Martha Stewart herself would be proud of—is that what she was doing when I heard her bawling her eyes out late last night?

Tyler scoops a heaping spoonful of the tuna casserole onto his plate, deftly balancing his beer bottle between two fingers. Craning his neck to see into the living room, his eyes are fixed on the obscenely large flat-screen TV where horses are being corralled into the starting gate at Santa Anita.

I look back to him, watch as he lifts the fork to his mouth in slow motion. A few noodles dripping with that hot mayonnaise concoction fall back to the plate as he opens his mouth wide and shovels what's left on the fork into his gaping pie hole. Chew, chew, chew, swallow and repeat the process again. By the time he takes his third mouthful I've got a white-knuckle grip on my own fork, poised and ready to stab the love of my life.

I don't love you anymore.

And once I say this in the quiet of my own mind, I know it to be true.

Tyler has been my *other* other half since we started dating back when we were sixteen. He was the captain of the basketball team, I was the head cheerleader. My first boyfriend, my first everything.

I try to go back there. I do. I try to remember what it was like when everything was shiny and new, when he was golden and full of promise. The way his cheeks would redden when I'd catch him looking my way. His friends pushing him so that he stumbled forward and right into me when he was too shy to ask me to homecoming. Our first kiss standing on my front porch in the rain. Dancing to *Copperhead Road* under those purple string lights his mother hung outside their trailer, half-drunk and happy in a way that made us both lightheaded. I remember the thrill of him holding me close. And that first time with Tyler, whispering *please* when he asked me once and then again if I was sure.

But Tyler's gone nuts like so many of the men in this ass-backwards town, with their get rich quick schemes and dreams of easy money. Since that casino in Powell opened up, I'd venture to guess that a good one-third of the homes in this county have gone into foreclosure or are damn near close to it.

My father always liked to bet the ponies. I remember him sitting in his recliner watching the races, and the special dinners my mother would make before the Preakness or the Kentucky Derby, right down to the virgin mint juleps she served us girls. We even took a family trip to New York once, alternating nights spent on Broadway with day trips out to the track to see the horses race in person. It's not like I have a lot in terms of world travel to go on, but I still look back on it as the best vacation of my life.

Wicked and *Mary Poppins*. I'm impressed that my parents were able to swing tickets for two Broadway shows back then. I mean, we grew up in a house and never wanted for anything, but we lived a modest life in a small, modest town. I remember eating dinner in some fancy Italian restaurant after seeing *Wicked*, my mother and father stifling their laughter while shushing me and my sister every time we broke out into song.

Everything about that week in New York was magical:

sipping on Shirley Temples, trying bites of baked clams and baked Alaska, spinning in circles taking in the lights, the costumed characters and the over the top themed shops of Times Square. Even those day trips we took to Belmont created lasting memories, good ones. Cigar smoke mixed with the smell of sauerkraut, the jockey's bright colored silks, the excitement when the bugle sounded the warning and the gates opened with a loud snap-clack.

And they're off!

Back then it was all in good fun. My father would ask his "best girls" which horses to bet on, and we'd make our picks based on which rider had the most colorful outfit or the horse with the kookiest name. We screamed our heads off rooting for our pick, and more often than not my father would toss his stubs to the ground, smiling as he said something like: *That's what I get for betting on a horse named Candy Cane Lane.*

I was busy with my own life, with the day-to-day drama of high school that's oh so important when you're in the thick of it, so I didn't notice the subtle changes.

I didn't notice until much later that his empty beer cans were taking up most of the real estate in our recycling bins, didn't notice the envelopes with *PAST DUE* stamped on them until my mother gave up hiding them, and didn't notice that my father was changing before my very eyes, that he'd slowly but surely checked out.

The police said he was intoxicated a few nights ago when his car swerved into oncoming traffic, but is that all there is to it?

I haven't told Sienna yet. I don't know how to put a positive spin on what I've been digging through these past few days. We've lost our parents, isn't that bad enough?

We may be identical, we may be able to finish one another's

sentences and feel physical pain when the other is hurt, but we're as different as two people can be.

Sienna is the sail to my anchor. She's happy, maybe even a little flighty, and she sees the world through rose-colored glasses. I'm practical, no-nonsense, and maybe I'm even guilty of seeing people's faults before I see their strengths. Sienna's husband calls me the un-fun twin. And if I'm being judged alongside Sally Sunshine, otherwise known as Sienna, then he's right.

Yes, my sister is already married, and the two blissfully happy idiots—whom I love dearly—have a baby on the way. They were blissfully happy up until last week anyway, so I'm not about to go pouring any more salt in her wounds or crushing her spirit with more bad news.

Sienna doesn't need to know that covering the funeral and burial alone is going to put us into debt, and that's *after* we sell the house. My father refinanced the mortgage so many times to support his addiction that it's now referred to as being *under water*. There's no equity to be had. They'll be no auction at Sotheby's either, as my mother's jewelry has already been pawned off, and they didn't really have much of monetary value to begin with. No, Sienna doesn't need to know.

I can handle this.

Garth is holding her, rocking her slowly from side to side. Sometimes I want to shake the two of them, tell them to wise up and start making better decisions, but I have to admit they have something between them that Tyler and I never had and probably never will.

My brother-in-law works at a hardware store. He unloads the deliveries, stocks the shelves, works the register and gives out dubious advice to people who come in asking questions about their home improvement projects. He makes minimum wage yet has no concerns as to how he's going to support the family they've decided they're ready to start. My sister had aspirations of being a teacher, same as me, but I think she's wanted to be a wife and mother since we started playing house in preschool and she's never stopped. She got through one year of community college before she left to work full time as a receptionist at a dentist's office. She will make a damn fine mother, I have no doubts on that front, but I wish the two of them hadn't signed up for such a life-altering responsibility so early on.

I worry, they don't. They don't ask for much from this life, don't expect much, and while that makes me sad, I can't help but acknowledge that they are happy. Garth may never move them out of that trailer, he may never pay off the ridiculous truck he bought last year entirely on credit, but he does love my sister with his whole heart. I have to be grateful for that.

I turn away from the two of them, start clearing the paper plates and cups, nodding as I pass people who speak more words of sympathy and condolence. When I enter the kitchen I see Tyler in a corner whispering into his phone as he checks some paper that looks like the cheat sheets he used to rely on in high school.

I ask, "What's that?" even though I already know what it is. It's the point spread, the over-under, the puck line, the odds, the what the fuck ever. He's talking to his bookie, so sure about whatever sure thing he's got going that he'll risk my wrath.

He holds up one finger, smiling his sweet smile as he gestures for me to wait. I cross the kitchen, rip the phone from his hand and throw it against the wall with all my might. His mouth hangs open as he watches the phone connect and then fall to the floor in pieces.

I'm not afraid he'll fight back, yell at me or even get angry. Tyler is a good person. He's always been gentle with me, shown me in so many ways that he loves me. He would never set out to intentionally hurt me.

I used to love the determined look he got on his face when he played basketball. I'd whine about the hours he spent perfecting his free throw, but I secretly admired his work ethic and the devotion he showed to improving his skills. And he was something to see back then. The boy is and has always been drop-dead gorgeous, but on Friday nights in the gym he was otherworldly. Crowding the sidelines with the other cheerleaders, I swear I used to feel faint when he'd wink at me running back down court after hitting a three-pointer as just about every person in the entire gym rose to their feet and chanted his name.

But that was then and this is now. That drive and tenacity are long gone. He's hopped from one job to another, spewing nonsense about his big plans to open a sports bar while making no concrete moves to make it a reality. The boy has never even tended bar or worked in a restaurant. He takes his paychecks, cashes them, and then bets on a winner in the hopes that he'll be able to pocket a windfall to fund his dream.

He is sick. I get that now.

I also know that I don't have the power to make him change.

He won't change, and I'm not about to ride shotgun with him down this miserable road he's chosen. I've seen how this movie ends, and I'm getting out long before the final credits roll.

Chapter Two

SKYLAR

The letter I've been waiting on, the one I looked upon as a key with the power to open a door to some unknown but fantastic future, now sits crumpled amid the others. Those other papers, with their threats and warnings, have the power to close every door and lock me in.

It's worse than I thought. He didn't just gamble away the house and their savings. He didn't just leave tax liens, outstanding credit card and utility bills behind. Nope, he went all in.

Pardon the pun.

Searching in vain for some life insurance, for some long-forgotten rainy day fund—for anything to pull us out of the hole we're in—that's when I came across it.

My sister is the one who cries when she's sad, I don't. But last night I broke down and wept. Cried most of the night and got it out of my system. My eyes are puffy and red, I greet the rising sun tired, but the pity party is over.

I'm not mad anymore. I don't feel cheated or used. There's no time for that. I am cut off from feeling, I'm disconnected and numb.

My body feels cold, my thoughts are linear and focused, my movements take on a stiff and mechanical quality as I shift into problem-solving mode and begin sorting the papers into piles. One for the collection agencies, one for the IRS...

I can't sit and dwell on the fact that my father took our social security numbers, mine and Sienna's, and opened multiple accounts in our names. No, I have to block it all out so that I can fix it. So instead of going online to start the process of registering for the fall semester, I'm now typing phrases into my outdated laptop's search bar, looking for ways to untangle this mess.

It's shocking, and it's no comfort to know that my sister and I are not alone. There are lots of us out there. Identity theft. Credit card fraud. I knew it happened, just never imagined that parents were so often the culprits. If I wasn't staring at the papers right now, the proof in my hands, never in a million years would I believe that my father would set me and my sister up like this.

I reach down to the floor and grab the letter, smooth it out against my thigh. I guess I'm not all out of tears because one lands with a splat, turning the admissions director's signature into nothing more than a sad inkblot.

Dear Skylar Perillo,
We are pleased to offer you a seat as a transfer student
into the University of Pittsburgh this coming fall.
Your academic achievements have earned you a merit
scholarship in the amount of...

The letter drops from my hands again and I fall back onto the couch.

"What's the matter?" my sister asks, rushing over to me looking scared out of her wits.

I gesture to the floor, incapable of speech because I can't make sense of what I'm feeling right now.

Sienna is jumping up and down, clutching the paper in one hand and rubbing her still-flat belly with the other. "You got in! Oh my God, you got in!" When I don't respond, she looks down at her belly and says, "Did you hear that? Your brilliant auntie got herself a scholarship!"

"I can't accept it. I can't leave."

Garth comes up behind her and places both hands on her belly while resting his chin on her shoulder.

"Why?" they ask in unison.

Their cluelessness knows no bounds. I look around, waving my hands at the stacks that clutter every surface, the folders and papers that lay on the floor. "There's too much to do."

"School doesn't start for two months." Sierra smiles at me and nods. "We'll get this all sorted out before then."

"Sienna..."

I don't want to tell her. I don't want to wipe that sunny, hopeful look off her face. It's the first time I've seen the girl happy in days. But no, I can't keep this from her.

I walk over to the stack of bills, the ones with the mounting finance fees and penalties, and fish out the two with her name on them. "Don't freak out," I tell her. "I think we can get this cleared up because the accounts were opened without your consent, and the charges...Well, I don't think it will be hard to prove that Dad wasn't looking to better your life since just about all of the charges are for on-line betting sites."

Her mouth hangs open as she skims each page and then hands them to Garth.

"I read up on it last night. If the charges were for tuition or clothing or something else that could be looked upon as supporting you, then it would be a different story. But this looks like a clear case of identity theft."

"Daddy?"

I can't do anything but nod my head. I hold back from calling him every bad word I've learned over the course of my life because what good would it do?

I'm too tired to be mad. And I'm too sad. This is the same person who perched me high up on his shoulders so I could see the world, who taught me to line dance and taught me how to drive.

How can you hate and love and miss someone, all at the same time? I want to scream at my mother and father, and at the same time I want to press my face into the fabric of that ratty old couch where they'd sit watching *Wheel of Fortune* every night just for the scent, for the memory of them.

I have no parents. No grandparents still walking this earth. No aunts or uncles I'd refer to as family. But I do have Sienna. And I have Garth. I feel so alone yet so grateful for them.

"I can't leave. You'll need help with the baby."

"Skylar, now more than ever I'm convinced that you need to do this. You don't need to take care of me." She looks over her shoulder and smiles softly at her man. "And Garth's mother is here to help us with the baby."

"Yeah, she can't wait to be a granny." He moves in closer, puts his hand on my shoulder. "And you need to get away from here."

"Away from him, you mean?"

"I love that kid like a brother but he's still acting like he's seventeen and he's got all the time in the world to get his act together." When I crack a smile, he frowns. "I know what you think of me. I know you think I'm nothing but a fuck up—"

"No, Garth!"

He silences me with one hand. "I know you think I'm a dreamer. Is that better?" He doesn't wait for me to answer. "But we've got this. Me and Sienna? We'll be the best parents any kid could ask for. I can take care of this family."

I feel like crap on a cracker. I know in that moment that the advice I dish out on a regular basis and my well-intentioned offers to "help" have probably come off as condescending. Like I'm superior. Like I've got it all figured out. Yeah, right.

"I love you, Garth. You *are* my brother, and I know you'll take good care of Sienna."

"Then trust in this." He tussles my hair as my sister wipes at her eyes. "Go and do all those great things you've always dreamed about."

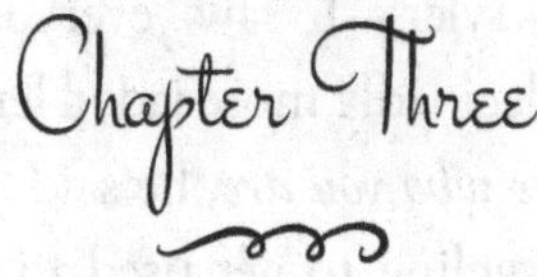

Chapter Three

SKYLAR

Six weeks later, legally bankrupt and basically homeless, I'm standing on the steps in front of Tyler's place. His mother and father still pay the bills but spend most weekends out at his grandparents' old fishing cabin just over the state line.

I knock a second time, thinking back to how convenient it was, the way Tyler's parents were always taking off for the weekends. We shared a lot of memorable nights here. He threw the biggest parties, some of them lasting from Friday night well into Sunday afternoon, and we had some great times here alone, too. Cooking together, watching movies on the couch side by side, *not* watching movies. We played house, played at being adults.

He puts on a face like he's annoyed when he sees it's me at the door, but I know him, know there's way more hurt than anything else involved when it comes to me.

I felt like an assassin a few weeks ago when Tyler doubled

over like I'd landed a shot to his gut, like I'd physically knocked the wind out of him.

He never saw it coming, and how could he? I was a different person the day after the crash. I saw my mother, my father, my town, Tyler—I saw everyone and everything through a new and decidedly more jaded lens.

I don't even know who you are, he said. And I felt the same. Fact is, I'm still struggling to get used to this new version of myself. I'm still on the fence as to whether or not I even like her.

He promised me he'd change, begged me not to do this to him, begged for another chance. He cried but I didn't. I was stone-faced and distant, treating the break-up as just another box I had to check off on my very long to-do list.

Standing across from him now, I feel the weight of what I've done to Tyler. I've never had the power to hurt another person the way I've hurt him, and there's no pleasure in having the upper hand.

I'm leaving tomorrow. I'm driving my late-model Sentra up to Pittsburgh and starting a new chapter. So today is for making amends, for closure.

They say it's easier to leave than to be left behind, and I believe that. But when Lila Watkins comes sauntering out of Tyler's bedroom, making her way to the kitchen so she's sure to be seen, I'm the one who feels like I've been sucker punched. I hand over the cardboard box with what I'm sure is a lifeless expression because I feel dead.

For a fleeting moment I imagine them tangled up in his sheets. Does he make her laugh, blow raspberries on her naked skin and tickle her even though she begs him not to? Does he study her and smile as he runs one hand through her long hair? Does he tell Lila how beautiful she is?

He looks over his shoulder to see what's got my attention and then turns back to me. Taking the box from my hands, he says, "You didn't have to give this stuff back." When Tyler adds, "It's just crap," I don't know if he's referring to the tattered blue flannel I used to wrap myself up in, or if he's referring to us, to me.

I want to tell him. I want to tell him that what we had was special. That I'll always have nothing but love for him, always want good things for him. But she's here. She's wearing one of his shirts with nothing on underneath, acting like she belongs. And his eyes, eyes that were always soft and smiling, are hard now and taking me in like I'm nothing more than an unwelcome guest. He shifts on his feet, impatient.

I turn to go. "Take care of yourself, Tyler."

He clears his throat, and when I look back he's running his thumb back and forth over his chin as if he's trying to decide something. A moment later he gives me a sad, lopsided smile that I return. He doesn't need to say it and neither do I.

He calls after me, "Good luck, Sky."

I turn back to thank him but he's already shut the door.

Chapter Four

SKYLAR

Less than an hour.

That's all it will take whenever you want to drive back home, take a break, go and see Sienna.

This is what I tell myself whenever I feel lonely, which is basically all the time.

My scholarship covers everything—tuition, room and board. There's no way I would have been able to come here otherwise. I can't apply for a school loan, and any landlord with half a brain wouldn't rent to me after getting a look at my credit score. Nope, I'm a cash and carry girl now. I have a bank account, but I'm not allowed things like overdraft privileges and such. I won't be in the clear until my credit record is expunged, and I'm told that could take a while.

It's fine, I tell myself. It could have been worse. Walking into the police station and filing a report was humiliating, but we got through it. Wes took the report, a guy only a few years older than me, and he damn near choked on his coffee when

Sienna named our father as the perpetrator. My father, a perp. The thought of it, picturing him in his button-down shirts and pleated *slacks*, as he still called them—he couldn't look more straight-laced, upstanding and ordinary if he tried.

Wes was good about it. After that momentary lapse in professional conduct, he took our information with a straight face, nodding impassively and acting as if people came into the station every day claiming their father had put them into debt for close to a hundred thousand dollars.

That was the worst of it. Dealing with the FTC was a piece of cake in comparison. Those government agencies do, in fact, deal with this sort of bullshit on a daily basis. So the woman who was handling our case may have been shaking her head in sympathy and clucking her tongue in disapproval on the other end of the phone line, but at least we didn't have to witness it like we did walking out of the precinct.

By the time we left, it was obvious that every single officer knew our tale of woe. And the clerical worker, an old friend of my mother's who sat her ass on our couch for book club or Ladies' Auxiliary meetings more times than I can count, gave us nothing more than a weak smile as we passed her desk on the way out. She couldn't even look us in the eye.

But being the town pariah, charity case du jour, the object of scrutiny and sympathy—none of it matters to me. It's still home and I miss it.

I want to run home all the time. I don't like living in the dorms. My roommate is fine. It's not her. She minds her own business and keeps to herself. She's what I would have called a loner back in high school before I up and joined their ranks.

That's what has me so rattled. I used to be in the center of it all. I had friends, I had Tyler. And I didn't have to *make* friends. Nothing took effort. When you grow up in a small town like mine, everyone just knows you. You don't have to present this package to the world, let them open you up and then decide if you're worth keeping. You're just surrounded by the people who have known you, accepted you and loved you since day one. At least I felt that way.

This is like walking through a movie set every day. Life is going on all around me but I'm nothing more than a prop in the background, set dressing, silent and inanimate. Spirited conversations, the complex nonverbal language of relationships —even the most basic exchanges, like the man in line ordering his coffee as I sip my tea off to the side—I take it all in. I watch their body language, listen to their words, create imaginary backstories for each and every character.

I feel invisible.

I sit in these arena-style classrooms with upwards of three hundred students packed inside, but cannot seem to find one person to so much as make eye contact with. The five or ten minutes before classes start are the worst. Clusters of students talk, laugh as they look at some nonsense on their friend's phone, or walk into the room searching for a familiar face, smiling when they catch sight of their person.

I tell myself they've all been together since freshman year. I'm new here, a transfer student walking into a social scene that's already established. I tell myself to just give it some time. But this kind of isolation is unnerving. No, it's damn near paralyzing for an identical twin who's never once known the quiet solitude of being alone.

I call Sienna every afternoon. I call at around five, when I know she's home from work. She puts me on speaker while she makes dinner for Garth, and I find myself asking her to describe each step of the process in detail. We both love to cook, but this intense interest I have in their supper has more to do with the fact that I want to keep her on the line for as long as humanly possible.

I need to hear her voice. She knows this. She knows I'm lonely without me having to say it. So she walks me through each step as she makes some new chicken recipe she saw on *Pioneer Woman*. She regales me with stories about the most mundane details of our small-town life. She tells me who came in for a cleaning at the dental office that day, tells me who got engaged, who's getting divorced, and tells me who they ran into when they were out shopping for a new television the day before.

I bite my tongue and refrain from telling her that they can't afford a new television with a baby on the way, sticking to the pact I made with myself to butt out and stop criticizing their decisions. But damn, old habits die hard.

Sometimes she feels like one half of my body, my brain, and I am the other half of hers. But that's not how it is. Sienna is separate from me, a married woman soon to have a family of her own. And as much as I tell her in the quiet of my own mind that she needs to grow up, maybe it's me I'm talking to. I'm the one who needs to grow up, to let go and let her live her own life.

So now when we start heading for choppy waters, like tonight when she starts talking about the big Christening party they're planning to throw at some cheesy catering hall one town over—totally out of their budget—I change the topic.

I usually ask her about the pregnancy because I want to be there, standing next to her and holding her hand at every check-up, but Garth is there by her side as it should be. But I do love hearing about it afterwards, about the heartbeat that sounds strong and healthy, and about every new weird and fascinating change her body is undergoing.

Tonight I lay back on my bed, resting my hand on my own flat stomach as she describes the fluttery, light feeling of the baby stirring inside of her.

Alone in my room, it's moments like this when I'm at my weakest. After we hang up I stay there, imagine Tyler's hand caressing that spot and looking up to my face with wonder in his eyes.

"I love you," he whispers.

I could have that. I could have the comfort of my old life. We'd live just down the road from Garth and Sienna, be the foursome we've been since high school. We'd spend the weekends hanging out together and grilling dinner on Sunday afternoons in our yard or theirs. Raise our children together and be a family.

In those moments I don't dwell on the money troubles we'd surely have, or the arguments over his gambling. I see things like they used to be. A dreamscape of jumping off the rocks into the river, Tyler holding me close and rubbing my shoulders to ward off the chill after splashing into that water. The air darkens as the scene changes to nights of kissing in his car, of clothes being shed. Heavy breaths between him asking if it feels all right.

I don't know if I miss him or if I miss the comfort of being in a place where I'm known, where it's easier.

I've never been one of those people who curse small-town life. I've never had this pressing urge to bust out of some imaginary cage, but I know people like that.

Simon, a boy I used to crush on in high school even when I was dating Tyler, he used to talk about getting out of our town like it was ground zero for some deadly, flesh-eating bacterial disease. I could never understand it.

It's the opposite for me. I'm comforted by the familiar faces

I see every time I pop into the grocery store or the diner. I like when people greet me by name and ask after my family. Although people generally avoid that sort of talk now, you know, since the scandal, tragedy, or whatever people refer to the crash as. But things have slowly started to return to some semblance of normalcy. People ask about Sienna, about the baby. They congratulate me on the scholarship and wish me well.

I'm going places, they tell me. But am I? Leaving home, getting that degree I've held in such high regard, what will it do for me? I've always pictured myself standing tall and accomplished with that diploma in hand, but will it be that way? Will it make me happy or will it make me feel like an alien in my old life?

I imagine myself with one foot firmly planted in my past, and one foot in this new world, the terrain uneven and hard to navigate.

I don't know where I belong.

Chapter Five

SKYLAR

"Sienna?"

I stop in my tracks and turn to see who's calling after me. Yes, it's my sister's name, but I've always answered to both, same as her.

I can cut my hair in a different style, wear make-up, adopt far-out fashion trends to differentiate myself, but it's no use. We are identical in looks, mannerisms, the way we walk and the way we laugh.

"Jeez, you've got long legs. I've been chasing after you for the past couple of minutes." One of my favorite teachers, Miss Dawson, is flushed and smiling at me. "What are you doing here?"

I stop myself from reaching out to hug her because I'm pretty sure it will come off like a drowning person grasping for a lifeline. It just feels so good to see a familiar face, especially hers.

"Hi!" I let out on a squeak, my arms stiff at my sides but my smile matching hers.

"Skylar! Damn, I still always get you two confused."

I shrug, still smiling like a loon. "It's no biggie. We're used to it."

She gives me a quick once over before asking, "So you're a student here?"

"I just started. Transferred in as a junior in September."

She nods her head in approval. "That's fantastic! How's it going so far?"

People ask all the time. Friends from home, my student advisor, Sienna. I always chirp back, "Great!" or if I'm feeling especially plucky, "I love it!" But I can't seem to muster up the energy required to lie to this woman.

She was my English Lit teacher way back when, and she also ran a creative writing seminar. Miss Dawson would leave these thought-provoking comments on my papers, things that made me dig deeper or maybe examine my motives. I always believed she had some internal bullshit detector or something.

"It's all right."

She lets out a soft laugh. "I hope they don't hire you to lead campus tours for incoming freshman." When I don't respond she reaches a hand over to cup my cheek, and that alone nearly reduces me to tears. "Everyone goes through it, Skylar. Even the kids who are walking around smiling and laughing like they've got the world on a string. It's an adjustment."

I nod and clear my throat, embarrassed by the pathetic impression I'm making. "It's just so different from home. But it's only been six weeks. I'll get the hang of it."

"Are you on your way to class now? I just met up for coffee with a friend, but I'm kind of starving and could use a glass of wine. There's a cute little brick oven pizza place just a block off campus if you want to grab an early dinner."

I try my best but can't contain my enthusiasm when I nod my head to take her up on the offer. Share a meal with another actual human? Engage in conversation? Sign me up.

She fixes me with a knowing look once we're seated. "So tell me what's really going on."

I go to speak just as the server comes over. Miss Dawson smiles at the girl and orders two glasses of Cabernet. When she turns to go, Miss Dawson asks me, "Are you even twenty-one?"

"I will be in," I pause to do the math, "two weeks and one day."

Her eyebrows knit and then she smiles. "Halloween. That's right. I remember your senior year of high school…Your party was the talk of the town."

I shake my head. "We took advantage every time my parents went away for a night. But they were pretty good about it when they found out."

Her expression changes at the mention of my parents. Her smile is soft when she says, "They probably knew about the party all along. I mean, hell, I even knew about it." Tilting her head to the side she says, "I remember being surprised that you were eighteen a year before everyone else." Laughing, she adds, "Two of the tallest girls in the school."

"You're forgetting about Marcy Price. She dwarfed us. But yeah, with the whole preemie thing and being twins…My mother thought we'd be better off if she held us back. You should see our kindergarten picture."

"Taller than all the boys?" she asks, laughing.

I nod. "It's me and Sienna standing together in the center of the top row."

"We'll toast to your birthday tonight then." She lets out a

breath and smiles. "I'm an awesome role model. I went and ordered your underage butt an alcoholic beverage and didn't even ask if you like red over white, or if you even drink at all."

"Everything I know about wine is from watching cooking shows, but I like to try everything."

The server sets our glasses down and asks for our order but we haven't even looked at the menu yet.

"Is there anything you don't like, Skylar?" When I shake my head, she goes ahead and orders us a pie with brussel sprouts, pancetta and ricotta, and another with sausage and broccoli rabe.

"Sounds good."

"Trust me. You'll be daydreaming about this pizza from now on."

"Do you come up here a lot?"

She sips her wine and then shrugs. "Once or twice a month maybe? My boyfriend is a professor here."

"What department?"

"Humanities. Jack teaches philosophy."

"I wouldn't know him."

"What are you majoring in?"

When I answer, "Education," we both smile. "I'm concentrating on Early Childhood, though. I don't think I'm cut out for dealing with obnoxious teenagers the way you are."

"It can get pretty crazy in high school but I guess that's where I'm meant to be." She takes another sip before placing her glass down on the table. "He doesn't get it either. He wants me to move up here and get an adjunct position, settle into academia."

"But you don't want that."

"No. I deal with burnout every so often, but I love what I do. He has a point, though. I guess it's always good to have a back-up plan." That pensive look is gone, her eyes now smiling with mischief as she leans in and whispers, "Especially since those old crows on the school board are always grumbling about getting me fired."

"Still?" I shake my head when she nods. "They're idiots. I'm seriously not blowing smoke up your butt when I say you were the best teacher I've ever had." She raises her eyebrows and laughs as I take another sip. "I'm not tipsy. Not even close."

"Then thank you for the compliment." Miss Dawson lets out a breath. "I had to order new uniforms for the girls this fall. Those adorable spangled numbers were apparently too provocative."

"The red, white and blue ones?" When she nods, I add, "I loved those outfits. Our uniforms were lame compared to them."

"I always wondered why you were a cheerleader instead of focusing on dance. Nothing wrong with cheer, it's just that you're a talented dancer. I'd watch you doing the routines with your sister in the gym sometimes."

The server comes and sets our food on the table, and I'm glad for the break in conversation. I love dancing, always have, but I held back from doing anything Sienna was involved in when we were in high school.

As kids we always played the same sports and were on the same teams. I played piano, so did she. I mean, it made more sense in terms of arranging activities around our parents' schedules, but it reinforced this idea that me and Sienna were one in the same.

"Since you watch cooking shows, I'll go out on a limb and assume you're a foodie."

I take a slice of the white pie. "I make this one at home myself, except I use pancetta instead of prosciutto."

"Where on earth can you find pancetta in our town? Seriously, I'd think you'd have to sub in deli ham and green beans for this recipe."

We both bite into our pizza simultaneously and moan. Then we laugh, and I almost cry because this connection, this feeling of friendship is so good.

She raises her glass to mine. "I'm so glad I ran into you today."

"Me too."

"So?"

"I'm getting there. I think transferring in as a junior is what's making me feel so out of the loop."

She considers this, takes another bite, sips her wine and then looks at me. "You've also been through a devastating trauma. Let's not leave that out of the equation." She reaches across the table and takes my hand. "I'm so sorry I wasn't there to attend the funeral. Jack and I took an extended trip over the summer. I went to see you two when I heard the news but you were both gone, moved out. I know Sienna is still in town." She looks guilty when she adds, "I have to reach out to her."

I squeeze her hand, wanting to reassure her. "It's all right. We've been getting through it. And Sienna is doing really well. She's—."

"Having a baby." Her look is somber. "I heard."

"I mean, she's married. It wasn't some unplanned, out of left field situation. But I get it. I was a little disappointed when they told me too."

She rolls her eyes. "Listen to me, like I have all the answers." She reaches for the other pie, slides a slice onto my plate and then hers. "He was always a nice kid, Garth. I just hope she doesn't regret it."

Shaking my head, I can't help but smile. "That's the thing with the two of them...They're so damn happy I don't think it would ever occur to either one of them to think they were trapped, or that life had passed them by."

"Sienna was always a star-gazer, and I mean that in the best possible way."

"Garth is the same."

She tips her glass my way and then drains the last drop from it. "Then here's to them. Maybe I need some of that blind optimism. Maybe you do, too."

"So...Jack?"

"His name is actually Jaxson," she pauses, "with an x." She leans in and her eyes light up. "Which kills him, by the way."

"Why?"

"He fancies himself a serious academic, but he's been saddled with a name right out of a teen drama or a bad reality show. He'd prefer to be a Theodore or an Arthur, or maybe even a Thaddeus."

I giggle, the wine now doing its work. "So he goes by Jack? That doesn't exactly give off the philosopher vibe, now does it?"

"Nope. But in the eyes of other people, at least that nickname affords him the possibility of being named John, a solid old-world name. Or even Jackson spelled traditionally, like he's descendant from some established southern family."

"He could change it legally."

"I'm sure that's crossed his mind." She sighs. "I'm making him out to be ridiculous and he's not. He's a good man. We're just at a crossroads, I guess."

I nod, even though I'm not really sure what she means.

Miss Dawson seems as young and bubbly as she always has. Back in high school all of the boys crushed on her. She barely seemed old enough to be a teacher, but when you sat in her class there was no question about who was in charge. No one ever dared to make a crude comment or to challenge her in any way. And who in their right mind would want to be on her bad side? No, she had so much positive energy that you wanted a piece of it, for some of it to rub off on you.

"But enough about me." She signals to the waitress for some water. "Do you think maybe you have too much time on your hands? I know classes can be tough, especially when you're balancing a full course load, but maybe a part-time job or joining a club would help?" Before I can answer she breaks into a seated full-body groove. "Maybe joining the dance squad would be just what the doctor ordered."

I look around to see if she's making a spectacle of herself, while it's obvious that she couldn't care less. I need some of what she's got.

"I have a work study job in the education department office, but it's only eight hours a week. That's all I qualify for since I have a full scholarship, which is bananas. I'm not exactly a Rockefeller."

"And what about dance? It would be a great way to meet people."

Feeling more hopeful than I have in weeks, I nod. "Yeah, I'll look into that." I look down for a moment, fiddle with my napkin in my lap when I say, "I always wanted to dance in high school."

"Oh my God! What stopped you?"

"I made this dumb pact with myself when we started freshman year...No more twinsies. I'd be different. Sienna took Spanish, I took German. She stayed with piano, I took guitar even though I hated it. Sienna joined the dance team, I became a cheerleader." Looking back up to her I add, "I mean, we were basically joined at the hip otherwise, so there was really no point."

"Look on the bright side. You now sprechen sie deutsch and play guitar."

A laugh escapes. "Um, no, I don't deutsch sprechen. You got that translation wrong but I'm hardly any better. I barely got through that course. And I can only play the opening chords of *Smoke on the Water*, same as every other failed rocker."

She channels Madonna. "But you can dance."

"Yup." I find myself imitating her ridiculous seat dance. "At night, I lock the doors so no one else can see."

She throws her head back and laughs. "I'm coming to the recital this spring and you better be up on that stage."

I sound ballsy to my own ears, accepting the challenge. "Maybe I will be."

On the sidewalk outside, she hugs me close and I do the same, feeling like I just got a shot of much-needed adrenaline.

"Hey, in a few weeks I told Jack I'd go to some faculty benefit concert thing with him. They're boring as all get out and he usually abandons me to kiss up to the department chairs, but sometimes the music is good. Want to come? You'd be doing me a solid."

Being that I have absolutely nothing on my social calendar, I accept. She takes my number and I program hers into my phone.

Before she turns to go, I hug her again and thank her.

"For what?"

"For dinner and...For everything."

Part Two

~~~

IT'S HARD TO BE A SAINT IN THE CITY
~~~

Chapter Six

SKYLAR

I'm here twenty minutes early. It's become routine.

I like practicing in front of the mirror for a little while before the rest of them show up to start stretching. I'm rusty and I don't like feeling as if I don't belong.

None of them make me feel that way. This is just a club, not a bona fide dance team or anything. But still, it's easy to see that most of them have been enrolled in dance classes since they could walk.

A few like to dance as a way to let off steam, same as me, but the majority are hard core. I find myself looking up terms on my phone after practice or texting Miss Dawson. They go something like this: *Kick ball change? Um, hello?*

I think she's loving this as much as I am. She reminds me that she's coming to the spring show, making it sound like a threat. There's a performance right before Christmas break, but I'm pretty sure I won't have enough rehearsal time under my belt to even make it onto the stage for that one so I'm keeping it to myself.

"You're not blowing us off again tonight, are you Skylar?" Pilar walks into the studio—make that glides in—and sets her bag down on the floor next to mine.

"Um..."

"Nope, nada, no way." Her boyfriend Devon shakes his head. "Last week you promised, so no more lame excuses. I want to see that fine ass out on the floor," he turns and winks at his girl, "and so does Pilar."

Pilar, Devon, Isadora, Misha—they even sound like real dancers. I'm even more sympathetic to Grace's boy Jax than I was before. This crew reads like the lineup of principal dancers at the Bolshoi. And while Skylar Perillo doesn't exactly read *working the pole*, it doesn't have the same ring as say, Simone Carrington, just another one of the insanely talented dancers in this group.

"If she doesn't want to go, leave her alone." Simone always sounds like she's bored, so when she's talking about me it's unnerving.

Isadora sits between me and Pilar to start her stretching. "Simone doesn't want you stealing any of her thunder. She thinks she's Beyonce once she gets out on the dance floor."

"Oh, I'm not afraid of any competition from you slags."

"Slags?" Pilar teases. "For the one hundredth time, you're not British. You're from Cleveland, remember?"

Once I stand, Devon comes up behind me and gets me going in a slow samba step. "Come with us. You look like you need some fun."

And he's right. So after practice I rush back to the dorms, take the quickest shower known to mankind, and slip into the only thing I own that just might pass for club attire.

There are no clubs where I'm from. There are a few bars that have line dancing on Friday and Saturday nights, but those are even considered out of town. The majority of my dancing has been done at house parties, where jeans and a tight top are considered cosmopolitan, so getting into a cab in high heels and a minidress feels downright foreign.

I'm in the dorm that houses scholarship and foreign visa students, so none of my dance troupe friends are nearby. And while I'm not usually one of those people who can't walk into a party alone, right now I'm wishing I would have arranged to meet Pilar and Devon outside.

Standing on the sidewalk at the address they provided, there's nothing to indicate that I've arrived at the right place. It's dark out here and the building looks like some old abandoned factory. I was expecting, I don't know, a red velvet rope, a few beefy bouncers—something to indicate that I'm not on the set of some horror movie.

I text Pilar: *Are you here?*

Yes, she writes back. *Thought you were flaking out.*

I'm here, I think. But...

Before I can type anything else, Misha pushes open the warehouse door and the pulsing beat of dance music fills the air.

"Devon told me to come get you. We forgot you've never been here before."

"Oh my God. I thought I got the address wrong or something. I was expecting—"

"Studio 54 circa 1978?"

I don't answer because I'm not sure if he's making fun of me or not. Odds are that he is.

"C'mon, you'll love it. The DJ is a friend of mine." Wrapping one arm around my waist as he leads me inside, he leans in and whispers, "And you look smokin' hot."

Mischa is not into me, I'm one hundred percent certain of that, so I take his compliment and the fact that he insists on buying my first drink as kind gestures meant to make me feel more at ease. I feel like a fish out of water right now so I must be looking the part, too.

"I didn't peg you as a martini girl."

"This is the first time I've had one. I'll let you know how it goes."

Taking my first sip, I do my best to hide the fact that it tastes like poison going down. People seriously drink these for pleasure?

Mischa laughs and squeezes my hip. "Just think of it as liquid courage." He points towards the center of the dance floor. "See where we are?" I nod when I see a few familiar faces. "Have a few more sips of that and then come join us."

I nod and then watch as he makes his way back out onto the floor as if he owns it. And once he gets back to his boyfriend, the two of them begin to move together in this perfect way, as if their bodies are channeling the music. A mash up of one of my favorite Artic Monkeys songs with Harry Styles' *Woman* is playing. The beat is slow, pulsing and hypnotic.

As the song blends into another track, Simone wedges herself between the two of them and they become the sexiest threesome I've ever seen—make that the only threesome. Misha's hands are caressing Simone's hips, and his boyfriend is pressed in close behind her body. It's beautiful, and hotter than any choreographed routine because this is natural—it's second nature to people who were born to dance.

Absently sipping on my martini, which I can't say tastes all that bad now, a tap on my shoulder breaks me out of my trance. I didn't even realize I was moving to the music until the man leans in to whisper, "I like the way you dance."

"Um, thanks?"

He looks me over from head to toe, his attention making me so uncomfortable that I gulp down the last few sips of my drink. I only register the basics on him: tall, dark and handsome, expensive smelling cologne, and a vibe that makes me wary.

"Can I get you another drink?" Before I can tell him no, he orders another martini from the bartender, a dirty martini. I don't even know what that means but it doesn't sound good.

"Hey, um, no thanks. I'm here with friends and I'm good, really. But thank you."

He looks to the bartender behind us who's doing some elaborate gestures with the martini shaker. "No pressure. But he's already made them, so just let me enjoy having a drink with a beautiful woman and then I'll send you back to your friends."

Skylar Perillo on a normal day? When I say no, I mean it. If anyone tried to override me or boss me around on my home turf I'd laugh in their face. But the confidence that always came naturally to me just isn't there lately.

The bartender pours the martinis and I take mine directly, knowing enough not to let this stranger handle my drink. I take a few polite sips as he makes small talk. He asks my name. I lie. Where I'm from. I lie. And the effort it's taking for him to keep this up is like pulling teeth, so I think he's actually relieved a few minutes later when I tell him I have to get back to my friends.

I walk away from him laughing to myself, giddy from the alcohol and just pondering the absurdity of this whole big city mating routine. We are a bunch of wild animals out here in the night. Dressed to impress, faces painted, everyone struts their stuff in the hopes of landing a partner. And looking down at the high heels I've only bothered to strap myself into once before, I have to acknowledge that I'm no different from the rest.

As I make my way to my friends, pressing myself between writhing, sweat-slicked bodies, the thumping beat of the track lulls me. I'm shaking my hips like Shakira, and don't even realize it until Pilar starts whooping and the others join in and grab me into a sweaty group hug.

"I'm so glad you made it!" she yells over the music.

"Me too!"

Sounding downright genuine, Simone says, "And you look hot."

I breathe a sigh of relief when I see the dress she's wearing is similar to mine. I never questioned my fashion choices before, but now I'm pretty much always second-guessing myself.

"I like your dress," I tell her.

She rolls her eyes and leans in so I can hear her. "We look like twins. Next time we'll have to coordinate better."

And when she pulls back I see that she's smiling. Aw, see that? She's not a bitch after all.

Simone takes one of my hands and Pilar takes the other, and soon we've formed our own hot little threesome. The vodka has definitely worked its magic. I feel free and uninhibited, and I throw my head back and laugh when I notice that people have made a circle around us.

The strobe lights flash on and off, changing colors and

making the people around us seem as if they're disappearing and then reappearing over and over again.

The way we're moving makes it impossible to really study anyone, but I can register eyes that express interest and some that are predatory. Out here I don't feel like a helpless minnow surrounded by sharks, though. No, when I'm dancing I feel powerful.

Chapter Seven

LEO

What am I doing here?

That's what I'm asking myself as the driver pulls up outside the abandoned warehouse Max has assured us is the hottest new club in the city.

One Friday night a month I allow myself some downtime. One night a month away from my job, my research, my home, my daughter—from the responsibilities that sometimes feel like they're weighing me down.

I wouldn't change a thing about my life because of Olivia, but sometimes I feel like a hamster running on a wheel. So anytime I'm somewhere I don't want to be, when I feel like I'm wasting my time? To say that I resent it is putting it mildly.

But tonight we played cards at Max's house. When the weekly game is held at my place, it's cards, beer, game on the television in the background and that's it. Max is single though, and he makes no secret of the fact that he finds my life boring.

He's always angling to get everyone to make a night of it when he's hosting, and while a few of the guys are always up for an all-nighter on the town, I typically bail.

Our friend Jonah announced halfway through the game that he just bought a ring for his girl, and then proceeded to pull the two-carat rock out of his pocket to show us. So that's how Max guilted me into this.

I tell myself I'm having one drink and then calling myself a cab as we enter the dimly-lit space that's loud as hell. This was never my scene, even for that brief period of time when I was young, single and believed I had the world by the balls.

And as I sip my whiskey, only half listening to my friends' conversation, it's not hard to recall why I always preferred townie bars. I like drinking beer, listening to good music and watching whatever playoff game happens to be playing on the big screen television. I don't like it here. The guys are all dressed like Armani models, while the women look like painted versions of their real selves, complete with fake eyelashes, hair extensions and fake tits. And while I used to like to dance, I hate the thumping techno crap that's playing in this place.

Max abandoned the rest of us within ten minutes—surprise, surprise. I can see him out there now with some woman. No, make that two. I'm not old, I'm only twenty-nine, but I feel like I'm fifty all of a sudden. I'd like nothing more than to enjoy this whiskey from the comfort of my own home, sitting in my worn, oversized leather chair.

"You think I'm making a good decision?"

It takes me a second to realize that Jonah is directing this question my way. "About what?"

He chuckles and shakes his head. "About getting married."

"Sure. I mean, do you love her?"

"Yeah." He nods once and smiles. "I do. But it's a big step. I can't really talk about it with Max even though he's my best friend. He just doesn't get it. He likes Lauren and thinks she's cool, but he doesn't get me wanting to spend my whole life with just one woman. I know with you...Your situation was complicated and all, but what's it like, marriage?"

I take a long pull off my drink and Jonah mistakes this for anger. "I'm sorry, man. Shouldn't have brought it up."

"No, it's all right. I just...Maybe I'm not the right guy to be asking. My marriage was..." It was, it was—it's something I still can't bring myself to talk about. "But I do know happily married people. My parents are married thirty-two years and they're still going strong. Like two halves of one good, solid unit. It exists, you just have to find the right person, I guess."

Find the right person. Who am I to be doling out advice? I don't know shit. "Want another?" I ask him as I turn back to the bar.

"I'm good," he answers, and a moment later he taps me on the shoulder and points towards the door. Two girls come walking in, and the one who makes eye contact with Jonah looks as hopeful and sparkly as a brand-new penny. "That's her."

I can't help but smile when I see the looks that pass between them. It is out there, I guess. As pessimistic as I may be, I do believe in true love. Just my crap luck that I didn't find the right girl.

I excuse myself and go to the bathroom when Lauren's friend starts making a play for me. I'm just not in the mood. I tell myself I'll say my goodbyes and then head home, knowing I'm more than slightly buzzed already. All this marriage talk had me swilling drinks at a way faster pace than normal and I'm feeling it now.

When I get back to where we were standing, the others are

gone and it's just Max with two girls. Not the ones he was dancing with before. He hands me another whiskey and I groan. "I have to be up at the crack of dawn, Max."

"Live a little, Grandpa." Turning to the girls, he says, "Ladies, this is my friend, Leo." He doesn't bother to introduce them by name because I'm sure he doesn't know them.

"Hi, Leo. I like that name," the one closest to me says.

She doesn't offer her name in return and I don't really care. She's attractive, I guess. Any other normal person would say that she's hot—I know this—but I've been having a hard time mustering up anything close to interest or initiative in that department for some time.

The other one already has her arms wrapped around Max's neck and she's whispering in his ear. When the music changes, though, she pops her head up like a poltergeist and screams, "I love this song!"

"C'mon," she corrals the rest of us, "we're dancing to this one."

I have no idea what this song is. To me it sounds like all the others, but it must be popular because the floor is packed. Whatever, I'm lazy now and let her lead me out onto the dance floor as Max's babe takes him by the hand and does the same. It takes me a minute or two to get into it, but my new friend is bumping and grinding enough for the two of us right off the bat.

I find that I'm not loving this, but maybe I am liking it a little. I'm taking in everything around me and remembering the way I used to be. I take in the scent that is unmistakably feminine, losing myself in that combination of sweat and heat and sweetness. And now she's got her arms wrapped around my neck and her body pressed into the grooves of mine. I'm enjoying the feel of it, but it's more like an out of body sensation, a memory.

This girl is yelling above the music into my ear. I can't really make out what until she says something about Cirque de Soleil and then laughs as she looks to the group of people behind her. She must have thought that's where my attention was focused, and while it wasn't before, it is now.

There's eight, maybe ten of them clustered together. The women are mostly long and lean, a few are curvier, and the guys aren't dressed like the finance-bro set. No, they're more artsy. And once you look, you can't look away because these people can move. I get what this chick was saying, they do look like performers, but she said it as a dig, like there's something staged and ridiculous about them.

I see nothing but sex.

I see bodies moving in perfect rhythm.

I see sweat rolling down one girl's neck.

I see hips pressed back against her man's eager body.

Oh, that's *my* girl pressing her ass against my body, but I'm not eager for her and don't want her thinking that I am. I go to move her forward, gently, and turn to make my way back off the dance floor. I don't want what she's offering. Nothing good will come of it. She looks back to me pouting as I mouth the word *sorry*.

I get one step away, then two. Wading through the crush of bodies is like trying to race walk in chest-deep water. I'm passing by that group when one of the girls trips over herself and falls right into my arms.

"I'm so sorry!" she calls out over the music.

"It's all right. You steady now?"

She smiles and laughs, has that same purity and happiness

radiating from her like Jonah's girl. She's tall, maybe five-eight or nine, but I still tower over her. I'm smiling for no reason whatsoever as I turn to go, but at that moment the music changes again and my tipsy dancer raises my hands in the air and then proceeds to do something that looks like a pole dance with me acting as the pole. I had no interest whatsoever in my last dance partner, but I'm finding this girl's act hot as hell.

Speechless, I move along with her as my eyes rake over her body. Her legs are long, exposed in all their glory by the short dress she's wearing. The fabric hugs her body tight, shows off her pert tits and her round ass.

She's moving her head from side to side, eyes closed, lost in the music in a good way. I put my hands on her hips, follow her motions and then can't help but draw her in closer. She responds by turning slowly, and unlike before, when *this* girl's ass is pressed up against my crotch I find that I'm not inclined to protest. Not even a little. She takes my hands from her hips and guides them over her belly and lower before arching back and lacing her hands around my neck.

"You like that?" I lean down and ask her, knowing she can feel me hard against her backside.

"Yeah." It comes out on a raspy breath. "Feels nice."

It feels more than nice on my end. I haven't been this turned on in God knows how long. High-quality porn with the volume muted is the closest I get to real live action nowadays, so having this beautiful woman's body pressed up against mine is sensory overload. Every time she shifts her hips I feel like I could blow.

I lean down again, nuzzle into that spot below her ear and breathe her in. I love the scent she's giving off, can't get enough of it.

When she shifts her long hair to one side to give me full

access, I pull her in closer, grind myself against her and lick the side of her neck like an animal. And thankfully she likes it because I'm torn between my desire to bite her earlobe and wondering if I've lost my damn mind. I want to be with this woman more than I want my next breath.

# Chapter Eight

SKYLAR

He just licked my neck. And not like a little slip of the tongue. The man flat-out feasted on my skin from my collarbone up to that spot right behind my ear.

I'm too drowsy and he feels too good for this to raise any concerns. I'm loving the way his big body envelopes mine when he holds me, love the rough calluses on his hands, and I'm flat-out ready to strip him out of his shirt so that I can get a better look at the ink that's covering the corded muscles of his forearm.

I want to turn and face him, to see *his* face, but he has me locked tight against him now and I don't want to do anything that will interrupt this perfect moment.

God, I've missed this. I've missed being touched, missed being worshipped the way Tyler all but knelt before me. I imagine it's him behind me for a split second but then decide I like the anonymity of this stranger's touch better.

But I'm not too far gone to know that this is not my reality.

I'm torn between my desire to just let go and the warning bells starting to go off inside my head. That voice is telling me that I don't do stuff like this. I don't hook up with guys I don't know. I don't let unfamiliar hands dig into my hips and then roam north to skim that sensitive spot just below my breasts. *But oh my*, I think as I drop my head back and succumb, *it feels so, so good.*

The music changes to some fast-paced EDM track, and while the people around us pick up the tempo, I stiffen just as he steps back. I should turn around, say goodbye or thank you or something, but I don't. I slip through the crush of bodies, grab my bag, walk as quickly as I can to the exit and escape.

The cold air hits my face, my arms, my legs. It's started to mist a little but the icy droplets give me some much needed relief.

I'm praying that he's not right behind me as I call for a car. Not because I'm afraid of him—I mean I should be but I'm not—but because I can't face the person I was with him back there. She was bold, sexual, adventurous. And while it was fun to walk on the wild side for a hot minute, I don't feel comfortable in that skin.

I've never been so happy to see my dorm, to clean the makeup from my face, to don my flannel pajamas, slip underneath my down comforter and fall into a dreamless sleep.

I silence my alarm and then shut my eyes against the memory of last night. I'm smiling to myself and cringing at the same time.

I'm not even the slightest bit hungover, so nothing about last night is a blur. And while I'm a tad embarrassed knowing that my new friends witnessed my dirty dancing routine, I'm giggling to myself more than anything. My dance friends aren't exactly prudes, and training with a partner kind of desensitizes you to the feel of skin on skin. They won't care. At most, I'll have to suffer through some harmless teasing. And that guy? I'll probably never see him again. No harm, no foul.

I may never see him, but lawd, I'm thinking of him. In the shower I let a soundtrack play in my head as I move the way I did last night.

Under the spray of warm water I let my hands roam where his did, from my hips to my ass to my breasts. I put the brakes on us last night, but now I'm fearless. Now I rest my head back against the tiles and I pretend.

I let him take what he wants and let him give me what I need.

Chapter Nine

SKYLAR

I'm the only student working in the office.

The position is split between several work-study students, and while kids are coming in here at all hours looking to speak to an advisor or to get answers to questions I generally can't answer, it's not really a placc to meet people.

I'm thinking this as I look at the four walls, replaying Miss Dawson's words. I need another part-time job. Maybe waitressing. I have experience with that. Maybe I can find a spot where the tips will be so good that I can leave this job where I make next to nothing.

Eight hours. I barely make enough money to keep myself stocked up on shampoo and tampons, forget about new clothes or luxuries like a salon haircut.

There's a big bulletin board on the wall in the waiting room with all sorts of announcements, and since I'm never really busy, I've got plenty of time to study it today.

My responsibilities in this office are limited to filing papers when the secretary asks, which she doesn't do all that often, and handing out course catalogs to the students and parents who come in. So I take my time scanning the concert flyers, the guide to campus mental health services, the ads looking for math tutors (not my subject) or foreign language tutors (definitely not my subject).

My eye catches on one post that's handwritten in bold block letters. You can see the ink has bled through the paper, making it seem as if the words were written with a heavy hand, or by someone who was seriously stressed out. I put my hand over my mouth, stifling a giggle as I make my way through the list of qualifications for this babysitting position.

-A <u>minimum</u> of two years' experience caring for a toddler.
-3.5 GPA <u>or higher</u>.
-Must be <u>Red Cross</u> CPR certified.
-EXCELLENT DRIVER WITH NO HISTORY OF ACCIDENTS OR SPEEDING TICKETS.

All caps for that last item. Whoever wrote this means business. And then right above the tabs with the phone number to call, you get one last parting shot:

-Must meet ALL qualifications (no exceptions) and must be able to start immediately.

I wonder when this was put up, and with a satisfied smirk I notice that not one single tab has been ripped off.

Babysitting? It's more like an ad for a position in the president's security detail, complete with background check.

And while I happen to tick all the boxes for this type-A,

neurotic potential employer, I have no intention of applying. Everything about it screams miserable helicopter parent.

No thank you.

I'm still smiling, scanning the board for something worthwhile when I feel a tug on the hem of my skirt. I look down to see the most adorable little thing looking back up at me.

I crouch down to her level and give her a big smile to calm that bottom lip of hers that's quivering. "My name is Skylar. What's your name?"

"Libby. I can't find my daddy." She starts to cry when she adds, "He told me don't walk away."

"It's ok, Libby. I'll help you find him." She nods and tries to smile through her tears. "Let's see...Which way did you come from?"

She looks back and forth like I do. The halls aren't crammed or anything, but there are a fair amount of people. I look down to see her still looking back and forth. She has no idea. I scan the hall again for a frantic parent but don't see one.

"Libby, you can sit at my desk while I get this sorted out. And don't worry, when I was your age I used to get lost all the time. We'll find your dad, piece of cake." I smile and snap my fingers before lifting her onto my chair. "How old are you?"

She holds up four fingers and says, "I'm four years old." I note that she uses *I'm four*, not *I four*, and make the uneducated assumption that she's bright. "And do you know your last name?"

"Libby Hale." *Hmm...A little difficulty annunciating the L, but pretty good.* I'm about to tell her to sit tight when she adds, "I live at 246 Grove Circle, Skwell Hill Nort, 15232."

Damn, she even knows her zip code. "You live in Squirrel Hill North?" She nods. "I love that name! Are there really hills with squirrels running all around?"

"Yes!"

Since she knows the zip code I go for the phone number, but she gets jammed up on the last few digits and then starts to cry again.

"No biggie, Libby. I don't need the phone number." I poke my head around the corner. "Diana," I call out to the department chair's personal secretary. "If Doctor Thompson comes back," I lower my voice to a whisper, "tell him I have a lost little girl in my office. I'm going to call the security desk and let them know."

Diana walks in as I'm on the phone with security. "And who is this little sweetie pie?"

Her tone surprises me in a good way, as this chick is typically all business. I might even use the word icy to describe her. But with Libby she morphs into gushing, smiling granny-mode, and it's not hard to understand why. Libby is all golden-curled, pink-cheeked sweetness.

Waiting on hold, I hand her a piece of the licorice I keep stashed in my bag, and her eyes light up as she struggles to undo the wrapper.

"Let me get that for you," Diana all but coos.

Libby frowns a moment later as she rips off a piece of the licorice with her teeth and chews. "I love candy but my daddy doesn't let me have any."

"That means he's a good dad." I perch my butt on the edge of the desk, wondering why I've been on hold for so long. "Candy is a special treat, not for every day."

Diana adds, "That's right, candy will ruin those little teeth of yours if you eat it every—"

We all stop in our tracks as the door practically flies off the hinges and some maniac barges into the office followed by Doctor Thompson and another man.

"Where's Olivia?" the big guy dressed in a leather jacket and jeans barks.

I manage an oh-so articulate *uh* as I point to Libby, while Diana goes all Momma Bear on him and stands in front of the child like a shield.

His face is red with rage. "Anyone think of maybe keeping her down by the front security desk?"

He's looking back and forth between me and Diana like he's waiting for an apology when he *should* be thanking us.

"I, I did call security...I'm still on hold."

"Well, while you've been *on hold*, I've been tearing through this campus looking for my daughter."

With that, Libby peeks her head out from behind Diana and says, "Hi, Daddy!" as if she doesn't have a care in the world and wasn't crying just a few minutes ago.

His expression changes in a heartbeat. The hard eyes and scowl are exchanged for a teary-eyed smile. Ok, he loves his baby. He's not a total dick.

"Olivia." He scoops her up and snuggles her close. "I told you to stay right next to me." He pulls back a few inches to look her in the eye. "Please don't ever do that again, ok?"

She rubs the stubble along his jaw with her little hand and pouts. "I won't. Promise."

He lets out a deep breath and looks to the man standing beside my boss. "Ed, walk us to the car so we can wrap this up. I don't have time to trek all the way back to your office."

Doctor Thompson, my department head, looks between Libby and his colleague, now known as Ed. "She made it all the way here from the engineering campus?"

Ed raises an eyebrow behind Grumpy Dad's back, as if to tell my boss: *Don't kick the hornet's nest.*

But it's too tempting, especially since this jerk still hasn't thanked us or apologized for the way he came barging in here.

"Four-year-olds need eyes on them *all* the time, right Libby?"

"Right, Sky." She smiles brightly, waving her floppy licorice wand back and forth at her father like she's scolding him. I want to jump up and high-five her for the way she delivered that line.

He lets out a *harrumph* as he sets Libby back down on the floor and takes her hand. "Time to go, baby." Giving us no more than a fleeting look, he says to her, "Say thank you to the nice ladies who helped us."

Libby breaks free from his hold and rushes over to me, wrapping her arms tight around my thighs. "Thank you, Sky."

I crouch down to give her a proper hug back. "You're welcome, Libby. You can come visit us anytime."

"What about me?" Diana whines, holding her arms out wide. "I don't get any sugar?"

I nudge Libby in Diana's direction, and Libby squeals and laughs when Diana squeezes her tight. "A hug is sugar?"

"Yep," we say in unison.

I look up to her father and see that his expression has changed again. He looks profoundly sad, or maybe I've got it all wrong. Maybe he's worried, anticipating the wrath he's going to face when Libby tells her mom what happened here today.

He looks on edge, that's for sure. And I would be too if my baby girl went missing for what was probably close to half an hour. The mathematics and engineering buildings are halfway across campus.

As the group walks out, he turns back to me and Diana, nodding his head once. I think that's all we're going to get but he surprises me when he says, "Thank you for this. You two saved the day."

Diana doesn't miss a beat, following after Doctor Thompson to relay his phone messages, but I'm spent. I let out a breath as I collapse back into my chair, trying and failing to make sense of the sadness that's suddenly weighing me down.

I feel the way he looked: crushed. But for the life of me I can't figure out why.

Chapter Ten

LEO

I grip the steering wheel tight in an effort to stop my hands from shaking. Olivia is chatting away, oblivious to the fact that I'm on the verge of a panic attack.

I keep picturing her, a tiny little thing walking amid all those big people, crossing pathways where campus vehicles make the rounds for sanitation and security. It's not like she crossed a major highway or anything, but she's four years old. I cannot believe she made it all the way to Foley Hall without anyone stopping her.

I push down thoughts of what could have happened, squeeze my eyes shut at a red light when an image of a man grabbing her and pulling her off to the side pops into my head. The person behind me lays on their horn startling me out of that nightmare, and I find myself talking myself down for the remaining ten minutes of the drive.

I let out a breath when we pull into the driveway, and

decide to have a talk with my little runaway while she's still trapped in her car seat.

"You scared Daddy today. Do you understand that?"

"Sorry, Daddy."

"Never...You can never walk away from me like that again."

"But I—"

"No buts. Something bad could have happened. Tell me you understand."

"Sky says she gets lost all the time."

That's one thing I can piece together from the ride home. She must have said the word sky at least twenty times. The girl's name is Sky. The one who found Olivia and kept her safe.

I acted like an ass, and she let me know it in her own subtle way. Yeah, thinking back on it I was rude, but she'll get over it.

I hated the way Olivia clung to her, latched onto her like an octopus. I hate that she attaches to strangers so easily. And that's what's really eating at me. I'm all she's got and I haven't been doing a stellar job. Between the shop, my workshop at home, and the occasional trips I make for business, I always feel like I'm neglecting her.

Today was a perfect example. Taking her to the engineering lab and expecting her to stay put while I talked shop with Ed for over an hour was the most dumbass thing I've ever done. *Don't sell yourself short*, my inner voice pipes up, *You do stupid shit like that all the time.*

The kid has no structure aside from the four hours of preschool she attends three times a week. Her mother, who was not exactly an authority on parenting, wanted her in all-day care from the time she was born but I wasn't having it.

The school she goes to now is expensive and selective, and they're all about not pushing full-time schooling until kindergarten. I agree with them in theory, but I'm doing a shit job of making her "exploratory time" enriching and meaningful.

In bed at eight, I'm yawning along with her as I read the last few pages of *The Princess and the Pea*.

"Is that Sky?" my daughter asks.

Long dark hair, warm brown eyes. I think back to earlier today and have to admit there's a likeness between the two of them.

"Do you think she looks like her?"

"Yes," she says with a sleepy smile. "Princesses are nice and they're really pretty. Sky is pretty and she's soooo nice."

Muffling a laugh, I ask, "So she must be a princess?"

"Yes," she answers on a yawn.

"Time for bed, little one."

I ease my way out of the bed, kiss Olivia's forehead and tuck her in. Her eyes are already closed, so I stand there and watch for a few moments. I silently thank that older woman and Sky again, and then make a vow to do better where my daughter is concerned.

Me and Libby against the world. It's always been that way.

Even when she was around.

I pick the frame up from Olivia's nightstand, look between the woman behind the glass and the spitting image of her lying curled up in bed.

Yes, my wife was pretty. I'll give her that. And that's all I needed at first, I guess. Just getting my business off the ground, I didn't really take the time to dig deeper, so I'm no innocent bystander in all this. Not even close.

I liked her on my arm, having her as my plus one. I liked falling into bed with her, appreciated her body and the way she moved with me. I just didn't know any better. Couldn't define the pit I always had in my stomach afterward when she'd roll out from underneath me, go into the bathroom and close the door. She never looked me in the eye, during the act or after.

We were burning out right around the time she came home drunk from a night out with "friends" and announced she was pregnant. And loving my daughter the way I do, I'm ashamed to admit that I hated her mother in that moment. I didn't say a word. Didn't have to. She studied my expression and said, "It's not like I want to marry you either, but I'm having this baby."

I used to blame myself. And she piled it on, too. She'd tell me *I* was the distant one, that I never had time for her, that I ignored her. And for a while there she had me going. So I spent the next seven months trying. Trying to get her to slow down and stop acting like she was still in college. Trying to see the good in her. Trying to ignore the late-night phone calls she answered, making excuses and accusing me of being paranoid when I pressed to know who it was.

Yeah, she was pretty.

But she wasn't nice.

Chapter Eleven

SKYLAR

I took the last of my midterms this morning, so I'm officially more than halfway through my first semester here.

Am I still homesick? Yes. Am I lonely? Sometimes. Do I still find myself pining away for Tyler? Hardly ever. And that tells me I made the right decision.

He's still with Lila from what I hear. Sienna doesn't offer that up and neither does Garth. That's strictly grapevine information, or what I gather from idly stalking their pages. It doesn't hurt, but maybe it does sting a little. I think there will always be some thread connecting me and Tyler, a first love kind of thing. But I'm pretty sure it's my friend who I'm missing, not my boyfriend.

Walking home after grabbing a post-dance practice beer with my friends, I'm as high as a kite. The endorphins from dancing for ninety minutes straight combined with that one light beer has me feeling euphoric in a silly way.

"Am I calling too late?"

Sienna laughs. "No, weenie, it's only nine o'clock."

"I just figured you might be tired."

"You're actually more tired in the first trimester. According to the book, I'm supposed to have boundless energy now that I'm in the second trimester."

"I can't believe you're halfway there already."

"I know. And when you come home for Thanksgiving next week you're going to be shocked at the size of me. I'm huge!"

"She looks great," I hear Garth call out from the background.

"Aw," we say in unison before laughing.

"It's going to be so weird, right?"

I nod even though she can't see me. "Our first holiday without them."

"I drove by the house the other day. It looks like whoever bought the place is taking care of it. There was a fall wreath on the door and pumpkins on the stoop."

"That makes me really happy for some reason."

"Me too," my sister says. "But you're sounding pretty chipper nowadays anyway."

"Was I a total Eeyore back in September?"

"Yeah. I'd get weepy every night after we hung up. I wanted to tell you to come home but I knew I couldn't."

"I'm glad you didn't. I would have been packing up my car and speeding back. I mean, it's still tough some days but I'm starting to settle in."

"Oh, I almost forgot! Miss Dawson popped in on us the other day to give her condolences and to drop off some baby stuff."

"She's the best."

"She is. She was the best teacher I ever had."

I nod my head again. "Same for me."

"Anyway, she told me you joined the dance club up there? What the hell, Sky…You've been holding out on me?"

"It's nothing. She pushed me to sign up so I'd meet some people. And whatever, it's turned out to be a good thing. I feel totally awkward because some of the girls *and* the guys…" I trail off, trying to think of a way to do them justice. "Sienna, they dance like they should be on Broadway. I'm serious!"

"I'm sure you're doing just fine. One thing I know for sure is that the Perillo twins can shake it."

"Damn straight," Garth says.

"Is he listening in on this entire conversation?"

When he says, "Damn straight," again, we both crack up laughing.

"I have period cramps, Garth. Any suggestions?"

"Hot shower followed by some hot sex. That always does the trick around here."

Sienna is laughing so hard she can't catch her breath. And shame on me, I should know by now that Garth doesn't get embarrassed or back down so easily.

"Being that the second half of that plan isn't an option, I'm going to say goodnight to you two freaks."

"Love you, Sky."

"Yeah, I love you guys too."

I walk along, smiling and laughing to myself. *Hot sex.* I don't think I've ever had sex that could be described as truly hot. I've given myself some spectacular orgasms, but Tyler? Hmm, I definitely enjoyed the journey to the finish line with him but he never got me all the way there.

He'd always finish first and pretty much collapse on top of me right after. I didn't have it in me to ask for what I wanted. It was just easier to call it a day, to pretend when he'd ask if it was good for me.

Lying in bed wide awake, long after my roommate's breathing evens out in a way that tells me she's down for the count, I slip my hand under my shirt and move up, cupping one breast and then the other.

I picture Tyler at first, but the image of him pressing his body against mine does nothing for me. Slipping my other hand beneath the waistband of my sleep shorts, I go with the image of a stranger. He's broad-shouldered, muscular and powerful. His legs are strong and his ass is firm. He towers above me, making me feel like I'm at his mercy. His hands are rough but his touch is gentle, and his words are kind and reverent. He tells me that I'm his, that I'm all he needs.

At a certain point I'm aware that my stranger has taken the form of that man, Libby's dad, otherwise known as Grumpy Daddy, but I ignore that inconvenient turn of events in my fantasy.

Grump or not, the man was hot, and right now he's giving me the absolute best oral I've ever had. I'm close, so close, but I still can't get there until I picture him bending me over the desk in my office and pounding me into oblivion.

I sound like I've run a marathon, and pull the blankets up over my head to muffle the sound as I come down from that blessed high.

Rolling over, now in a pleasantly hypnotic state, I giggle as I drift off to sleep. It may have been his face and his body, but the oh so lovely man in my fantasy was a big step up from that uptight jerk.

Chapter Twelve

LEO

"Maureen, you have to lighten up on the junk food, ok?"

An eye roll? Did she seriously just roll her eyes at me?

"Listen, I'm getting calls from school that her snack bag is filled with chips and sugary juice, and she's refusing to eat the food harvested from the school's garden."

"Harvested?" She snorts. "If you ask me, I think that school is a crunchy granola ridiculous nightmare."

"Nope...Didn't ask."

"So what am I supposed to be now, a babysitter or an organic farmer?"

"I'm just asking you to try to push the healthier stuff on Libby. I'm guilty of feeding her crap too, but I'm trying to make an effort."

"I saw your effort in the garbage can this morning. I'll go out on a limb and assume that broccoli was on the menu last night?"

"Salmon, too. And yes, while it didn't go over very well,

75

I'm not giving up. No more fries, no more chicken nuggets, no more mac and cheese."

"Good Lord. My kids grew up on that, and do I need to remind you that both of my sons went to ivy league schools?"

"First off, chicken nuggets weren't even around back then, and second off..."

"What?"

Nope. I'm not going to remind her that attending an ivy league school and actually graduating from said school are two entirely different things.

"Nothing. I just want her to be eating better foods. It's good for her."

"I'll try my best."

She says this with no conviction whatsoever.

Maureen is a salty old lady who is wise, kind-hearted and very set in her ways. And she's got me by the balls right now.

She's basically been my saving grace, the only person I've trusted around Olivia since her mother's been gone. She lives across the street, so the set-up is more than convenient, but it's not optimal. Libby is safe in her care, but that's because she plops her in front of the television and lets her watch cartoons all day.

And why the hell is no one responding to that ad I posted? You'd think college kids would be lining up around the block for a gig like this. I pay well, I'm easy to work for, and Olivia is a dream.

Maybe I should have asked Ed to post the flyer in every department, not just in the education building. But that feels like settling, and I don't want to settle where my daughter is concerned. I have this image in my mind of an aspiring teacher spending quality one-on-one time with my daughter.

Maureen is like the anti-Mary Poppins. There's no pep in

her step, she's undisciplined, and she's basically driving through her golden years on cruise control. And Maureen has already raised her own children. She's entitled, I get it. But I want better for Olivia. I want Mary Poppins.

I'll ask him tonight at that ridiculous fundraising event he conned me into attending.

Crap. That means I'll have to ask Maureen if she's available to babysit again. At least I can leave after Olivia's bedtime, that way I can be sure she won't be hopped up on ice cream watching television on the couch when I get home.

Yeah, the best laid plans and all that.

I had a crazy day at the shop working on a custom order to begin with, then had the added stress of being pulled in to participate on a few conference calls to trouble shoot problems with my team of engineers. I always feel like I'm being pulled in a million different directions, but with the race season gearing up to go, the pressure has been constant these past few weeks.

The chicken I planned to prepare is still sitting in the refrigerator raw, and the corn I was going to grill on the cob sits on the counter still wrapped in its husk. I took the easy road, swapped it out for mac and cheese. I remind myself that I did toss some frozen peas in while the pasta was cooking, but as I pull on my sports coat getting ready to run out on my daughter, I know I've messed up yet again.

"No ice cream, got it? No cheese crackers. No juice."

Maureen looks to Olivia. "Are you writing this all down, Libby?"

She's mocking me. Again. And I get it. She's told me straight out she's an old dog not looking to learn any new tricks. But seriously, is feeding the kid an apple and putting her to bed on time asking too much?

Sighing, I cave in like I always do. "Be good for Maureen, honey, ok?"

Olivia barely looks over her shoulder as she's opening the freezer in search of her mint chocolate chip ice cream. "Love you, Daddy. Bye."

By the time I get into the car I feel defeated. This is so damn hard. She's just one little girl. Why is this so complicated?

My mother made everything look effortless. She worked *and* had a good meal on the table at least four or five nights out of the week. As a kid I wanted for nothing. And unlike me, my mother never seemed all that stressed out about my schooling, my friends or my mental well-being.

I'm tempted to flip the guy behind me the bird when he honks his horn for the second time, but road rage is for morons and I know it's not him that I'm mad at.

I'm mad at her.

SKYLAR

"Wow, Skylar, you look like...an adult!"

"Is it too much?" I ask, pulling up the neckline of my black wrap dress. "I didn't know what to wear to this thing."

Looking at Miss Dawson's more relaxed, bohemian get-up, I decide that I do look out of place. The professors are in blazers and dress pants, not necessarily suits, and the women look chic but informal. I'm dressed like an upscale member of the catering staff.

"You look gorgeous. You can never go wrong with black."

I side-eye her. "Says Stevie Nicks." And she giggles at that one.

"I am a bit on the colorful side tonight, so I'll be the one sticking out." She tilts her head to the side. "Jack will not be amused."

"Can I call him Jax when you introduce us?"

"No!" She can barely contain her laughter now. "Although his reaction would be freaking priceless. And while we're on the subject, stop calling me Miss Dawson. You're not my student anymore and it makes me feel ancient. Call me Grace."

"You got it, Grace. So, do you have to come to these events often?"

"Not so much…Once every other month? I don't really mind it. I usually get to hear some great music or see a performance. Oh, and the stuffy professors Jack has to suck up to? Watching that scene reaffirms the decision I've made not to leave my job, so that's an added incentive to suffer through these nights."

"Why does he have to suck up?"

"It's all about tenure. Until you get tenure you're in limbo. And your future rests in the hands of these guys," she adds, scanning the room. "There are a few women too, but this is still an old boys club."

She turns when a man taps her shoulder and smiles down at her. "You're late, Grace."

"Jack." For all her teasing, it's clear in the way she looks at him that she genuinely likes him. "Sorry, I told Skylar I'd meet her outside."

With that, he looks to me and extends his hand as Grace introduces us. "It's nice to meet you, Skylar."

"Skylar is one of my former star pupils."

"I don't know about that."

Jack nods. "She doesn't hand out praise very often, so if she says it, I'll take it as is bible truth."

He takes Grace's hand, and I can't help but look down to study the way their fingers lace together, to watch as his thumb moves back and forth slowly over her skin.

"Skylar's an education major. She just transferred here."

Jack rouses me from my fog when he says, "Then welcome to Pitt."

"Thank you."

"So, education…What drove that decision?"

"I know it's a cliché, but I've wanted to be a teacher since I was in kindergarten. I remember playing school all the time when I was a little kid." Looking to Grace, I add, "And I had some fantastic teachers along the way who really inspired me. I want to be that person for someone else."

"It's a noble profession." He looks down at Grace and then winks at me. "She inspires me too."

Ok, he's too cute. I'm going to give it to Grace later on for making him out to be something that he's not. And I'm suddenly feeling bad for the guy. He does seem more like a Thaddeus than a Jax, and it must be awful living day to day in the hopes of impressing guys like my department chair.

Doctor Thompson is Grayson Thompson the Third, Ph.D. He's nice as far as bosses go, but now that I think about it, I've witnessed him being dismissive to the younger professors on occasion, giving off a vibe that's superior. Maybe these waters aren't so easy to navigate for Jax.

"Skylar, can I borrow Grace for a minute?" Looking to her, he adds, "I want you to meet my new graduate teaching assistant. She's great."

"Sure. Will you be ok, Skylar?"

"Of course. I've been eyeing that cheese board over there for the last five minutes. I'm going to go introduce myself right now."

Grace pinches my hip. "A dancer who eats cheese. You're my kind of girl."

I watch the two of them make their way across the room, watch as he taps another woman on the shoulder, watch the way Grace and the woman politely size one another up.

In my Human Behavioral Ecology class we study mating

behaviors in animals and the natural parallels between animals and humans. Some of the rituals are so bizarre. Male birds of paradise practice a complex dance taught to them by their fathers, perfecting it until that special day when they perform it in front of the females, all in the hopes of winning the dance off. Sage grouses puff out their chests, raise their tail feathers and whistle, hoping to stand out among the crowd and lure in a lady friend. And don't even get me started on giraffes. Just, ew.

Usually the guys have to work to lure in the ladies, but mimicking the mating ritual of the silverback gorilla, across the room right now two beautiful females are vying for the attention of one bespectacled, clueless male specimen.

Jack is smiling, seemingly pleased that his woman and his new co-worker do, indeed, have lots in common and are getting along well, but I'm studying their interaction from a different angle.

I watch as the graduate student straightens her posture when she greets Grace—possibly in a show of dominance—and she's been either consciously or subconsciously tilting her head to the side and smiling up at Jack whenever she addresses him. Grace, who is obviously no dope, has stepped closer to Jack and laced her fingers through his—a show of possession—and leans her head against Jack's shoulder right after he says something that's obviously complimentary—a clear demonstration of intimacy. New girl's expression drops when Jack laughs at something Grace says, and excuses herself a moment later.

Winner, winner, chicken dinner for Grace. And I shake my head in wonder after bearing witness to this theory playing out in real time. Nope, we aren't all that more sophisticated than animals after all.

"Skylar?"

I raise my hand to my mouth and speak around the mouthful of gruyere and grapes I'm chewing. Awesome. "Hi, Doctor Thompson."

He looks down at my dress and his brow wrinkles as if he can't figure out why I'm here. "Are you working this event?"

I knew I looked like the wait staff. "No." I brush the crumbs off my hands and try my best to look cool and composed. "I came with a friend. She's here with her boyfriend. He teaches in the Humanities Department."

"Excellent!" Hmm, he seems super happy to have cleared that up. "You know, it's an unbelievably odd turn of events. I was just thinking about you and it's like you've magically appeared."

"Really?" I'm kind of shocked that he even knows my name.

"If you don't mind, there's someone I want you to meet." And before I can say yes, I'm being led clear across the room. "You've actually met my colleague before," he says before approaching a small group. "Ed, do you remember this young lady from a few weeks ago?"

He studies me for a nanosecond before breaking into a wide grin. "I do! You saved the day if I recall." I return his smile but haven't a clue as to what's going on or who this guy is. "I'm Doctor Sheffield. I head the Mechanical Engineering program."

I shake his outstretched hand. "Skylar Perillo."

"Wait here, Skylar."

He shoots Thompson a smile and then goes to tap another guy on the shoulder. My cheeks turn a blazing shade of crimson when I come face to face with none other than

Grumpy Daddy, otherwise known as the guy I've used for inspiration the past couple of nights in my quest to get off.

Thompson says, "We were just discussing a dilemma Mr. Hale is having."

"Mr. Hale?"

He shifts on his feet before extending his hand. "Leo Hale. Olivia, uh, Libby's father." I smile and take his hand, letting him off the hook because he looks hella uncomfortable. "And I owe you a proper thank you...Maybe even an apology."

"It was nothing, and I'm glad it all turned out fine. She's an adorable little girl."

Thompson says, "Skylar, you actually came to mind when Mr. Hale was telling me about his difficulty in finding a babysitter. You did ask Diana for more hours, didn't you?"

"Yes, but...I mean, I was asking for more hours in my work study position."

He gives me a slick smile, which makes me question what the hell is really going on here. "Perhaps interacting directly with children would be more beneficial to your growth and development as a future educator."

Sheffield looks to his friend. "I'm kind of shocked you haven't gotten any responses to your ad. Hell, for what you're willing to pay I'd consider giving up *my* day job."

Grumpy, er, Mr. Hale shoots his friend a look. "Maybe I need someone older. If I haven't gotten any bites, maybe it's because undergrads don't have the kind of experience I'm looking for." He looks to me and adds, "No offense."

Something clicks into place, and before I can think better of it I blurt out, "That's *your* ad hanging up on our bulletin board?"

His tone is defensive when he answers, "It's mine."

I try to stifle the giggle that's pushing past my lips but it's no use. I'm picturing that ridiculous flyer, but now I'm hearing this stern, borderline angry guy ticking off each and every qualification. *No exceptions!*

"I could venture a guess as to why you're not getting any bites."

Thompson's eyes go wide while Sheffield cracks a smile and pats Libby's dad on the back. "Was it lacking in, say, civility?"

I look past Mr. Hale to his friend. "It was somewhat off-putting. You could say that."

Oh boy. Mr. Hale is mad now. "How is it off-putting? It's concise and direct."

I'm playing him now, because riling him up is fun, especially since I have *no* intention of working for him. "I was laughing when I read it. Would I have to submit a transcript, recent bloodwork, fingerprints and a DNA swab? I mean, requiring a 3.5 GPA and Red Cross certification for a babysitting gig is a little much, no?"

Thompson is looking a little horrified, and starts babbling like he's nervous or something. "I can personally attest to her qualifications in terms of GPA. Skylar earned a full merit scholarship as a transfer student from her local community college, and I know you need a near-perfect grade point average to qualify for that award."

"Skylar has always been a model student." Grace has joined us now. She's smiling at Mr. Hale when she adds, "And lucky for you, she worked summers as a lifeguard at our town pool." She snaps her fingers. "First aid and CPR certified to boot."

"Grace!"

She extends her hand. "My name is Grace Dawson. And you are?"

He takes her hand while I stand there like a bystander to my own life. "Leo Hale."

"Well, Leo, I can't think of a more qualified young woman for *this* job or any other." She's really laying it on thick and enjoying this entirely too much. "I've known Skylar for years, and as her former teacher I can tell you that she's a dedicated and hard-working person who also happens to be kind and caring."

"Stop. Talking," I whisper to Grace.

Sheffield is enjoying this too. "And we already know Libby would be over the moon." He looks from Hale to me. "She *still* hasn't stopped talking about you."

Now Jack has joined us, and he zones in on Thompson, obviously eager to make a connection with one of the department heads aligned with his program. Grace stands by her man's side to join in on the schmooze fest just as Sheffield excuses himself, which leaves just me and Mr. Hale.

Can you say awkward?

Looking to the ground, he stuffs his hands in his pants pockets. "I didn't realize the ad would come off as obnoxious."

"It's not that bad. And I'm sorry for poking fun, especially in front of your friends. You're just looking out for Libby. And even though it did make me laugh, I get it."

He looks around the room. "Not exactly my friends. Ed, kind of, but your boss is just another faculty administrator kissing up to me. He also chairs the Endowment Fund Committee."

"I didn't know that. I guess I need to personally thank him for my scholarship, huh?"

The big man finally cracks a genuine smile. "It sounds like you earned that on your own. So, are you really looking for a job?" When I don't give an answer right away, he adds, "It pays twenty-five an hour."

"Dollars?"

That's more than double what I make at my work study gig.

"Yes. But, uh, it is contingent on a few things."

"I'm listening."

"Do you drive?"

"I do." I immediately raise my palm to stop him. "And before you ask, I have no accidents or speeding tickets on my record."

He nods, jaw tight. "My hours are flexible, so we can figure out a schedule working around your classes, but I'd need a commitment of at least fifteen hours a week."

Did I say math wasn't my strong suit? Well, when motivated I can multiply pretty damn fast. Three-hundred and seventy-five dollars a week to babysit? Is he high?

"I can do that."

"Some weekend nights occasionally?"

"Sure."

"And," he rubs at the stubble along his chin, "this would be on a trial basis."

"Of course."

The amount of money he's dangling before me is unreal, but still, I'm thinking *he's* the one who will be on trial. Yes, twenty-five dollars an hour is a king's ransom for me right now, but let's face it, I'm not entirely sure this man will make a fair or sane employer. Maybe his last few babysitters quit on him. Maybe that's why he has to pay so much.

"Could you come by this Sunday so I can see how you interact with Olivia? I mean, I've seen you interact with her, but to tell you the truth I was half out of my mind by the time I got to your office. Oh...And I'll pay you for your time of course."

"That's not necessary."

"I insist."

"Ok then." I pull out my phone. "I'll give you my number so you can send me the address."

After he programs my number into his phone, he says, "See you Sunday at noon."

He turns to go, and I watch as he stops to shake hands with a few people and say his goodbyes. Meanwhile, I stand rooted in place long after he's gone.

What in the hell did I just sign up for?

Chapter Fourteen

LEO

I'm standing in the kitchen, looking around wondering what's the correct protocol for this odd job interview. Should I put out snacks, order some pizza? I tell myself no, that I'm not looking to impress this girl, but the truth is that I'm damn near desperate.

I came home a few nights ago after that fundraiser to find Maureen snoring on the couch with some obscene reality show playing on the television. And Olivia? She was wide awake eating potato chips next to Maureen, watching with rapt attention.

I had to take a few breaths to calm myself, because the truth is that I can't fire Maureen. So instead I carried Olivia upstairs as she wiped her greasy fingers on my dress shirt and then left salty crumbs in my beard when she kissed me good-night, went back down and turned off the television right before two deck hands were about to go at it in their shoebox-sized cabin, and then nudged Maureen's shoulder. She woke with a start, looking around to orient herself.

"What time is it?" she asked, rubbing at her eyes.

"Just about eleven."

She shook her head. "Just about an hour after you *said* you'd be home." Getting up off the couch, she yawned. "I'm past my bedtime."

I swallowed back my snarky retort because she was right, I did say I'd be home by ten o'clock. And maybe I shouldn't be asking a woman her age to work nights.

"What time do you need me tomorrow, Leo?"

"I'm taking the next few days off, so..."

"So call me when you need me." Smiling as she grabbed her sweater off the back of the couch, she looked to me cocking her head. "Oh, and we had apples with peanut butter for snack, just in case you were wondering."

I wanted to shoot back, *Was that before or after the Doritos?* But again I held my tongue.

"Honey, are you coming down? She should be here any minute."

I made the mistake of telling Libby on Friday that Skylar was coming over to see her today, and she's been asking me, "Is it Sunday yet?" ten times a day every day since.

I look up to the top of the stairs to see that Olivia has changed into her Halloween costume, a frilly pastel blue concoction that's no doubt fashioned after some Disney princess. It's still got chocolate smeared on it from last week.

Nice.

She's also made an attempt to do her hair with what looks like twenty sparkly clips tangled up into a rat's nest, and is that lipstick on her lips? Where the hell did she get that?

Right as I'm heading upstairs to get her cleaned up and looking the way she did twenty minutes ago, the doorbell rings.

Perfect.

"Uh, hi."

Her smile is practiced and uneasy as she returns my greeting and hands me a plate wrapped in plastic. "I like to bake so, um, I made carrot muffins."

"I love carrot muffins!"

Skylar turns in the direction of Olivia's voice and then covers her mouth to stifle her surprise. And she's good, I'll give her that, because I'm finding it hard not to laugh at my daughter in her current state. She looks like a slightly deranged, washed-up Hollywood starlet aiming to make an entrance as she saunters down the stairs.

"Wow. That's some dress, Libby."

"It's my costume."

"It's fabulous. And I like your sparkly clips." Skylar unclips one from the side of her own head. "I have these boring old brown ones, same color as my hair. Maybe I should get myself some of those."

"I think you should wear purple."

"Yeah, I like purple. Maybe you can do my hair someday."

I notice that Skylar's got a heavy bag slung over one shoulder so I gesture to help her with it. "What's all this?"

She barely gives me a passing glance as she hands the bag off to me, turning her attention back to Olivia when she says, "Just some stuff to play with. Art supplies, flash cards...Lots of stuff."

Olivia comes over and peers into the bag. "Do you have dolls?"

"No, but I bet you have some of those in your room, right?" When Olivia nods her head, Skylar says, "My sister and

I used to play school all the time when we were little. We'd sit our dolls up in chairs and pretend we were the teachers."

"I like to pretend."

"Me too." Skylar finally looks up and makes eye contact with me. "Do you want to play, too?"

Her question confuses me for a split-second before I understand that she's asking me how this is supposed to go.

"Uh, I have some work I need to get done if you two don't mind playing without me."

Olivia is already trying to sling Skylar's bag over her shoulder and lead her upstairs. "You wanna see my room?"

Skylar looks back to check and see if it's all right with me, and I nod my head once, feeling more than just a little uncomfortable. It's not that I don't trust Skylar, for some reason I instinctively do, it's just that I feel awkward. I'm in my own home, interviewing her for this job, and yet I'm the one who feels off-kilter. It's like I'm eager for her to approve of me when it should be the other way around.

I do have work to do, but I spend the next twenty minutes moving about the house restlessly, wondering what it is that I should be doing.

Should I be standing outside of Olivia's open bedroom door, watching the two of them interact? I felt intrusive the one time I paused in the doorway so I moved on, pretended I had to put in a load of wash. Going downstairs and totally being out on the action doesn't seem right either, and I certainly don't feel like I can plop down on the rug and join in on this game of school they've got going.

I settle on standing in the hallway out of sight like a creeper. And within two minutes I'm smiling, the sound of Olivia's laughter lighting me up from the inside. She's a happy kid by nature—it's not like this Skylar girl is performing some kind of magic trick by making her laugh —but I have to admit that I like what I'm hearing. Skylar is kind to my daughter, she's attentive and she's kind of goofy.

And seriously, my alternative is Maureen, so short of being an absolute mental case, acing this interview won't be all that difficult. Maureen has set the bar pretty damn low.

Poking my head in, I ask, "Libs, you want to help me with a snack? We can have Skylar's carrot muffins."

When Skylar unfolds her legs from underneath her and stands, Olivia follows. "Muffins!" she squeals as she grabs onto Skylar's hand.

It's a little embarrassing, the level of excitement Olivia is displaying. She's not just holding Skylar's hand, she's clutching it like she never wants to let go. But Skylar takes it in stride, going downstairs with her hand in hand, telling Olivia that if she likes the muffins then they can make them together someday.

"Do you want coffee?"

"I'm a tea drinker, but thanks anyway. Water is good for now."

"I want water, too."

I raise my eyebrows at this but don't question Olivia. I've been trying to reverse the bad habit I started when I swapped her baby bottle out for juice boxes a long time ago, and I haven't had much success.

"Good, you have a toaster oven. These taste so much better when they're warm with a little butter." Focusing on me, Skylar asks, "Does Libby have any allergies?"

"No. Ah, none that I know of anyway."

"Good. I was just thinking that back home I make this honey butter that can even make bran muffins taste incredible, but then I was thinking that, you know, honey, peanuts...I don't know if anything is off limits."

"No. I'm glad you asked but I think she's good."

"Olivia," Skylar's now crouched down, "you can get the butter out of the fridge and I'll warm the muffins." Looking up to me she asks in a way that's not really a question, "You're in charge of drinks?"

I nod and I obey.

Both of us do.

I'm at the water cooler, you know, the one that dispenses purified, crystal-clear water that comes from the most pristine mountain spring in Vermont. It sits in a corner and I haven't had to replace the bottle in ages because my daughter refuses to drink it and I've developed a nasty energy drink habit myself.

I'm beating myself up over the bad example I've been setting when Skylar's soft voice interrupts my internal chatter.

"What's up, hon? Having trouble finding it?"

I turn to see her standing next to Olivia, both of them peering into the refrigerator, but it's Skylar's ass that catches my eye.

The girl is beautiful in a way that would punch the air from any straight man's lungs. The other night at that university fundraiser, I spotted her from across the room. Didn't recognize her dressed the way she was, looking like one of the faculty, but I'm usually bored out of my mind at those events so I found myself watching her. She was going at the table of hors d'oeuvres like she hadn't eaten all day, which amused me at the time.

It doesn't say much about me that I didn't even recognize her until that simpering jerk Thompson practically dragged her across the room to meet me. Until we were face to face I'd been focusing on her mouth and the one hand she was using to fiddle with a pendant that fell right between the cleavage her low cut dress exposed.

I'm not a caveman but it's been a long time. So when a beautiful woman catches my eye, I look. I don't do more than that because my life isn't suited for meeting people, for dating —for anything that takes more precious time away from my child.

When Skylar turns to me with a tub of something in her hands and a look of pure disgust, I snap out of it and remind myself that I cannot do anything to screw this up.

"You use margarine? I didn't even think they made this stuff anymore." She turns back to the refrigerator, studying the contents for a moment. "Hmm...I guess the muffins don't need butter this time."

Once the three of us are seated, Skylar turns the tables on me and starts conducting the interview herself. I have to rattle off the name of Olivia's school, how many days a week and the hours she attends. Skylar nods in approval. When she presses me on Olivia's routine outside of school, I shrug my shoulders like I just got caught without my homework because in terms of routine, there's none to speak of. I'm wiped out by the time she asks about Olivia's favorite foods. My daughter takes over at that point, and I just basically sit there cringing as she rattles off her favorite picks from every drive-thru window in the greater Pittsburgh area.

Skylar is looking to me with wide eyes now, so I feel the need to defend the indefensible. "I don't have time to cook. And she, uh, refuses a lot of foods." Looking down to see Olivia picking up bits of shredded carrots and raisins off her plate, I feel especially ridiculous adding, "I wind up throwing good food in the trash when I make the effort."

She just nods her head, judging me in silence. I feel like

telling her to have at it because I'm in full agreement. Lab rats would turn their noses up at some of the stuff I feed Olivia.

"Do you know what my favorite thing to do is?"

My little girl's eyes light up. "Play dress-up?"

"Oh yeah, I *love* dress-up, but my *favorite* thing to do is cook. But the worst thing about living in my dorm at school is that I have to cook everything," she pinches her thumb and forefinger together for emphasis, "in a teeny tiny toaster oven. It's nothing like this beautiful kitchen."

As Olivia asks questions about this teeny tiny oven situation, I'm feeling pleased with myself as I see Skylar take in the six-burner Viking range, the Kitchen Aid mixer that's never been used, the Jura coffee maker, and the other ridiculously expensive appliances Olivia's mother demanded when we remodeled the kitchen.

"Mr. Hale?"

My wife never set foot in the kitchen once it was done to her exact specifications. Well, except for when she was uncorking some rosé from the Zephryr dual temperature-controlled wine refrigerator. Jeez, I think that alone retailed for fourteen hundred dollars.

"His name is Leo like a lion," Olivia corrects her.

"Uh, Leo?"

"Sorry, my mind drifted for a second there. What were you saying?"

"Just that if you don't mind, and that if I'm going to be coming by in the afternoons sometimes, I'd like to start teaching Olivia how to cook."

"She's four."

Skylar smiles. "I'm not talking cheese souffle or anything, just the basics. It's amazing the things kids will eat when they have a hand in preparing it."

"I love to cook!" Olivia says this while looking up at Skylar as if Snow White herself has landed right here in our very own kitchen.

I can feel the worry lines forming on my forehead.

What if Olivia gets too attached? What if this doesn't work out? What does this Skylar know about my baby? Nothing, that's what. She doesn't know that Olivia still cries for her mother, a woman she couldn't possibly have any memory of knowing.

"Be right back!" Olivia chirps as she scoots off her chair and heads for the stairs.

"Mr. Hale, I won't let her handle knives or leave her unsupervised. I just thought," she looks behind her to the counter where I've foolishly left out the selection of sugary cereals Olivia prefers, "you might want her to develop a love of good foods."

"Call me Leo."

"All right."

"And the cooking thing would be great. I haven't had much success in that department."

She looks back to the stairs. "Before she comes down, can you just give me a little background about your situation... Like, is her mother in the picture?"

"Does it matter?"

"Of course not. It's just that if she brings something up in conversation, I'd like to know what I'm dealing with."

I feel like I'm choking on the words when I answer, "No, her mother isn't in the picture. At all."

Skylar looks relieved to be done with that awkward exchange when Olivia bounds back into the kitchen full speed with something in her hand. "I did this. You look like the pea princess in my book."

"This is a beautiful drawing. I don't think I know the pea princess."

I clarify, "*The Princess and the Pea*."

Skylar's eyes go wide in recognition. "Oh, right. I used to love that story." Looking to Olivia, she says, "Maybe we can read it together next time."

"Now," Olivia decrees, looking to me as her humble servant. I guess this is where I'm supposed to hop to it and retrieve the book.

"Libby, your dad and I have to figure out what days I'll be coming to see you this week and then we'll plan what we're going to do then. Sound good? You want to look at the calendar with us?"

"Sure!"

Skylar grabs a sheet of paper from her bag and hands it to me. "This is my class schedule. I'm pretty flexible outside of that except for Thursday nights. I have a club practice that I can't miss unless it's an emergency." When Olivia starts looking through the set of alphabet cards sitting at the top of the bag, Skylar leans in and whispers, "I mean, I don't want to assume or anything but—"

"No, you're hired."

How's that for sounding desperate?

Looking over her schedule, I see that she only has one early morning class on Tuesdays. "Can you start this Tuesday? It would be great if I could get a full day's work in."

"Absolutely. I can be here by ten-thirty."

Feeling some absurd need to assert my authority, I tell her, "Tuesday it is, but I just want to make it clear that everything is still on a trial period basis."

She gives me a knowing smile, one that tells me she's fully aware that I'm up shit's creek but has decided to humor me.

"Did you hear that Olivia?" Pointing to the wall calendar she says, "I'm going to see you, not tomorrow but the next day. And we get to spend all of Tuesday together."

My girl whoops it up in her little voice and claps her hands, which damn near breaks me. *I can't worry about every little thing*, I tell myself. But it's no use. When it comes to my daughter, it feels like it's all I do.

Chapter Fifteen

LEO

I hardly ever check the thing anymore.

The first day she worked I was checking the nanny cam regularly, had the audio feed playing in the background all day as I tried in vain to get some work done. I listened in and caught myself smiling on and off all day as Olivia chatted happily, looking to impress this new person, and as Skylar listened patiently and then gently directed her charge through a range of activities that would have left me passed out on the couch.

With each passing day I paid less attention. I trusted Skylar.

By the end of the first month I was letting out a giant sigh of relief while praying this ideal arrangement would last.

Now nearly three months in, it's about as perfect as it can get, aside from a few hiccups. When I went to hand Skylar her pay in cash at the end of the first week, she looked beyond uncomfortable, insisting that it was too much. What she still doesn't realize is that I'd willingly pay three times that amount for the peace of mind her presence gives me. A wire transfer makes it less awkward for her, so that's what I've been doing. And the grocery thing was tough, but we got past that too.

She kept showing up with groceries, being that I don't have what you'd call a well-stocked pantry, and I didn't want her spending her own money. I felt guilty enough coming home to the most delicious dinners I've had since I was a kid living with my parents, so there was no way in hell I was about to let her shell out for the wild caught Pacific salmon she was buying. I told her I'd get her a credit card under my personal business account and register her as an authorized user. No big deal. But Skylar's eyes shot down to the floor, she shook her head and gave me a flat-out no without an explanation. I let it go, and a few days later she came clean and told me why she wouldn't be approved for a credit card once they ran her name and social security number.

I was speechless there for a minute, think I sank back down onto the couch but I'm not sure. This girl was now in my house more days a week than she wasn't. I'd come to rely on her and my daughter basically thought Skylar hung the moon. But I didn't know a thing about her. Not anything that mattered, anyway.

I didn't know Sky lost her parents just six months ago. Both of them at once and in such a tragic way—I felt sick when she first told me. But to lose your parents and *then* find out that your father had *stolen from Peter to pay Paul*, as she put it?

When I lifted my head from my hands and looked at her, she raised her chin in defiance and said, "My father was a good man. I know he must have been in a very bad place to do what he did."

Nope, I don't buy it. That's what I wanted to say. As far as I was concerned, her father was nothing more than a lowlife, a con man. His crimes unforgivable because he conned his family, his own children, the people he was supposed to protect above all else. But what good would that do? I could see in Skylar's expression that she was still wrestling with her own complicated feelings on the subject. She needed understanding from me and nothing more.

"I wish you would have told me."

"It's hard to talk about it."

"I get that, but I hope to God that you don't feel ashamed. Not in front of me."

"I used to be proud of my family." She was trying to be matter-of-fact about the whole thing, stoic, but her watery eyes gave her away. "I mean, we weren't like the perfect family, but we had a nice house, my father was well-respected, my mother had a seat on the school board. It's hard not to feel ashamed after everything gets stripped away and everyone can see all the ugly. And I guess I feel sort of ridiculous because I never saw it coming."

"I think lying becomes easier the more you do it. Some people get very good at hiding who they really are."

I know that from experience.

Leaning against the car I'm supposed to be working on at the moment, I'm thinking back to that night, remembering the way I wanted to wrap her up in my arms and give her some comfort the way a brother or a good friend would.

I go to pull up the app on my screen so that I can delete it. It doesn't feel right to have it anymore. I trust Skylar with my daughter, and don't want to give her a reason to ever think otherwise.

To be honest, there's a part of me that's a little bit afraid of that feisty girl too. I'm sure she'd understand. I mean, only an idiot would leave their kid alone with a caregiver they don't know without a way to check up on them. But what if she did find out about that camera perched on top of the refrigerator that gives a full view of the open-concept first floor? Would she flip her shit? Would she quit?

The app opens on my phone but before I can switch to settings, I'm drawn in by the sound of some God awful singing. Two off-key voices in tandem butchering Adele's *When We Were Young*. And I can't help but laugh when I see my daughter using a wooden spoon as a microphone to belt out her own version of the lyrics. "*Let me to-to-graph you in the light...*" Damn, she's adorable.

Skylar is singing along too, and then she breaks into a slow step, rocking her hips from side to side as she sings into a spatula, loud and off-key, just like Libs. It's comical, watching the way Olivia keeps looking up at Skylar and then trying her best to imitate her dance moves. But when my eyes drift and then fix on Skylar, comical and cute is not how I'd describe the show she's putting on. The girl may not be able to carry a tune, but she can move. She's not doing anything provocative. It's just simple and rhythmic, the way she's moving her hips back and forth. But damn, she has me close to salivating inside of a minute.

She's beautiful.

I imagine placing my hands on those hips, feeling the soft skin peeking out above the waistband of the jeans hugging her curves. With her free hand Skylar takes her long brown hair and moves it over one shoulder, and the gesture takes me back to my night out a few months ago, to that girl who ran out like Cinderella at the stroke of midnight.

But she isn't that girl, and as I switch back to the settings so that I can delete the nanny cam app, I mentally scold myself for thinking about Skylar in that way. I'm her employer and she is the most valued employee that I've ever had. I will not screw this up.

Chapter Sixteen

SKYLAR

"How do you feel today?"

"Same as I did yesterday...I feel like a whale."

"You look great, Sienna. Seriously, you can barely tell you're pregnant until you turn to the side."

Garth calls out, "And then it's like...Whoa!"

Thank the Lord Sienna laughs at this. My sister basically never gets mad at her husband.

I was just there visiting last weekend, but with her due date now less than three weeks away I'm checking in at least two times a day.

Some things will never change: I'm nervous, she's not.

"We have an appointment tomorrow morning. I'll call you if there's any news."

"Call me either way, news or no news."

"I will. I love you, Sky."

"Love you too."

"Do you love me?"

"You know I do, Garth."

I'm laughing as I end the call.

"Is the baby here yet?"

"Not yet, Olivia, but soon." I lead her over to the wall calendar. "See where I circled the day here, on the twenty-fourth? That's when the doctor thinks the baby will come. But the baby could come any day," I tell her as I drag my finger over the days in between now and the due date.

Olivia puts her finger on the day where we drew a red heart. "I want the baby to come this day."

"On Valentine's Day? Yeah, that would be great, wouldn't it?"

"Can I come see the baby?"

"I can ask your dad. I think he'll say yes." She's smiling from ear to ear. "And Sienna and Garth would love to meet you."

"I want a sister."

"Remember what we talked about?"

She looks down into the sink where the pots and pans sit soaking in the suds. "Every family is different."

"Yes, every family *is* different."

She's standing on a chair next to me, the both of us wearing rubber gloves. I smile thinking back to last week when Olivia ordered her father to wash the plate he'd just used, parroting my words: *Good cooks have clean kitchens.* I thought he was going to bust his gut laughing.

It's good to see him laugh, like to the point where it makes me feel all warm and tingly. I still can't say that I know him well, but I've collected bits and pieces of him along the way. In the very least I feel like I understand him a little better now.

He's brilliant, I know that much. Poking my head into the

garage he uses as a workshop one day, I was feeling sassy when I asked, "What do you do in here?"

He was taken off guard. Lifted the welding face shield up and stared at me for a long ten seconds or so before answering, "I build engines, like for cars."

"Oh. I thought you were an engineer."

"I am."

"A mechanical engineer like your friend, Ed?"

"Yeah, but I'm a mechanic first."

"Like, a mechanic who could fix my car?"

"I *could* fix your car, but I think it deserves to be put out to pasture."

I tried to smile because I knew he was just joking, but he sensed his misstep and apologized.

"No, I get it. It's a junker but I prefer the term vintage."

"Is it running all right? I'll take a look at it if you want."

"How in the heck would I know?" Gesturing outside, I teased, "You make me drive that monstrosity."

The monstrosity I was referring to is a new model Mercedes GLC complete with every available safety feature.

At first I was driving my car here, and then using the SUV to cart Olivia around, but Leo now insists on me taking the car back and forth to campus. He says that he can't be late for work in the event that my crappy Sentra breaks down or can't handle the winter weather, but sometimes I get the feeling that he's looking after me, taking care where I'm concerned. I'm sure it's just wishful thinking on my part.

Over the past few months I've pieced together that he's a great deal more than your everyday mechanic, or mechanical engineer for that matter. He also moonlights as a supervising engineer for a team on the professional racing circuit, and he holds patents for advanced technologies used in race cars, as well as regular old passenger vehicles.

The mechanic thing explains the rough skin on his hands and the speck-like stains underneath his fingernails that never come one hundred percent clean. And when I'm finding dirty fingernails hot, you know I'm hard up and my head is in a very weird place.

This man is my boss, but it's nothing like the kind of relationship you develop in an office. I mean, I've only held one office position so I don't know much, but the way I feel about Leo Hale is vastly different from the way I felt about my department chair, Doctor Thompson.

I'm in his home, I'm the one his daughter snuggles up next to on the couch, and I cook his dinner at least three nights a week even though he begs me not to. I do it under the guise of improving Olivia's eating habits, and while there's been major improvements made on that front, I also do it because I want him to eat well. He works so hard and he's juggling this parenting thing all alone. In the very least he deserves some good, home-cooked meals.

It took a few weeks for me to figure it out. When I asked about Olivia's mother and he said she was out of the picture, I assumed there was a bad break-up story involved. The words he used—*Her mother isn't in the picture at all*—at the time I was sure they were said in anger. But I read that wrong. She's deceased, so I'm thinking that was anguish and pain I heard in his voice.

I imagine it's a lot of pressure being a single parent. Add tragedy and grief into the mix and it's no wonder that grumpy is his default mode. He's not that way with Olivia, and I've seen him laughing with his friends when they come over to play cards just as I'm getting ready to leave for the day, but I imagine that he misses his wife and the sadness is a heavy weight to bear.

"Whatever you whipped up this time, it smells incredible."

I turn to see him walking in the door and watch as he pulls off his hat and coat. His cheeks are red and his hands look raw with cold. February is no joke in Pennsylvania.

"Don't you own a pair of gloves?"

"Yeah." Olivia wiggles her rubber glove-clad hands like she's channeling Beyonce in the video for *All the Single Ladies.* "You need gloves, Daddy."

He looks to her like she holds his heart in her hands. "You're right. Daddy should wear gloves. It's colder than a witch's, um...It's cold out there tonight."

"It's supposed to drop to ten below overnight."

"Is the heat in your dorm room working properly?"

"Please, it's always *too* hot. I don't know how or why, but even on a night like tonight it will feel like a sauna in my room. The second I get inside I'll strip down to a tank top and shorts."

He doesn't answer, and I'm turning red now thinking maybe that was TMI.

"Tell your dad what's on the menu for tonight."

"Cawafower rice, pink fish and beans amadee."

"That's right." I translate, "Pink fish, otherwise known as salmon, served over cauliflower rice with green beans almondine."

"I know I always tell you it's too much effort and not to bother, but I'm starving and this smells unbelievably good."

"Enjoy."

Walking to the foyer to grab my coat and bag, I'm just about to say goodnight when he stops me. "Can you stay and have dinner with us?"

"Um, I just figured you'd want some alone time with—"

"Stay, Skylar." Libby pleads in her sing-song voice.

"I won't feel good about eating this food knowing you're going back to eat at the campus dining hall. I don't remember the food being all that appetizing. It wasn't awful, but it wasn't like this," he says as he starts spooning food onto the plates I set out on the counter.

What the hell. It does smell great, and it's late, so the cafeteria will be limited to those fried chicken sandwiches and burgers at this hour. "Ok."

Libby puts a napkin down at each place and I get the utensils. We fill the cups from the water dispenser and sit down just as Leo puts our plates in front of us.

"Daddy, Sky showed me how to get bones out today."

"Yeah?"

I cover my mouth. "The salmon. I showed her how to use a tweezers to get the bones out."

"Nice. You're learning life skills, little girl."

Then he takes a mouthful and flat-out moans. And I want to moan right along with him because watching him eat is like porn for this sex-starved girl. Who knew that watching a man enjoy the food you've prepared for him is such a turn on? Hmm, maybe that's just my own personal kink.

We eat in peaceful silence for a few minutes, and when I allow myself to look at him again, I see that his eyes are fixed on Libby. Her table manners could use some work, but I don't think he's focused on that. I'm used to the fact that she's done a complete one-eighty where vegetables are concerned, but I think he's still taken by the sight of her munching on string beans or scooping mashed sweet potatoes into her little mouth.

"Good stuff, Olivia. Thank you, both of you, for cooking this delicious dinner."

"You're welcome," the two of us say in unison, and then Olivia breaks into a fit of giggles.

In the next moment, Olivia slaps her hand on the table and looks up to her father with a sudden sense of urgency. "Daddy, I can go see the baby. You say yes, right?"

"Oh." I wipe my mouth and then stand up to bring my plate to the sink. "Olivia asked if she could come with me one time to visit after my sister's baby is born. I told her we had to ask you first."

Libby puts a hand up to each side of her head, wiggles and makes a wide-eyed goofy face. "Sky said I gonna lose my mind when I meet her sister."

Now I'm doubled over laughing because she's freaking adorable, and Leo is looking back and forth between the two of us like we've already lost our minds.

"I showed Libby a picture, but it's nothing like seeing the two of us side by side. It freaks people out sometimes."

"I'm gonna be a mommy and have twin babies when I get big."

He coughs. "That's a loooong way off, little lady." Then looking to me, he asks, "You and your sister are twins?"

"I thought I mentioned it."

"No."

I pull my phone out of my back pocket and pull up the most recent picture of the two of us. Garth took it a few weeks ago. It's simple, just the two of us sitting side by side on the couch with our heads tilted in towards one another. I know who's who, but I realize that to most people we look like mirror images of the other.

Olivia wedges herself in between her father and the table. "See?" She's pointing to the screen. "They the same."

"Wow. Identical."

"Yep," Libby says, "not aternal."

"Fraternal," I correct her. "I was telling Libby about the difference because she has twins in her preschool class who don't look alike."

"Matthew and Meghan."

"Right," he says absently, still studying the picture. "That must have been different. I'd imagine it's a very unique way to grow up."

"I mean, I don't know anything else, but I suppose it seems strange to other people. Me and Sienna are definitely connected in a way that's more intense than traditional siblings...Like two halves of one whole. It's got some drawbacks I guess, but I wouldn't change it for the world."

He hands the phone back to me with a soft smile as his fingers innocently brush mine. I feel ridiculous, and look away to hide the blush creeping up my neck and across my cheeks.

If this man only knew the role he's been playing in my nightly bedtime routine. Thank God my roommate now spends most nights at her girlfriend's off-campus apartment. Her absence gives me the freedom to do as I please. And apparently, thinking about Leo Hale touching me is very, very pleasing.

I have to get out of here.

I reach for Olivia's plate but he puts his hand on my forearm, branding me yet again. "No way, Sky. You two cooked so I clean."

I like it when he says my name. Maybe a little too much. I can already see tonight's scene taking shape in my head. He'll be wrapping that same hand around my hair, pulling it back and over so that he can breathe my name into the skin of my neck as his free hand roams over my breasts, down to my hips and then lower still.

Ok, now it feels like it's topping one hundred degrees in here. He's too close, and I'm not known for my poker face. If he really studied my expression at the moment I'm sure he'd be able to read my mind and then the gig would be up. I'm suddenly finding it hard to keep my breaths even and calm.

I fetch my coat as he starts to clear the table, then walk back over to hug Olivia so I can make my escape.

"See you tomorrow, Sky-Sky," she says, hugging me back with an extra tight squeeze.

"No, Libs, remember? Tomorrow is Thursday. I have school all day and then dance practice."

"Aw," she whines. And I have to admit that I kind of love the fact that she misses me.

"I'm picking you up after school on Friday, so I'll see you soon."

I give her a peck on the cheek and then peep out a quick, *Bye, Leo*, as I turn to go, but something catches my eye. He's about to rinse the dishes before loading them into the dishwasher so he's pushed the sleeves of his thermal shirt up past his elbows.

One arm is a blank canvas while the other is covered from the wrist up. It's an eye-catching design, like a mash up between DaVinci's anatomy sketches and a futuristic cyborg. Cogs, pulleys and steel rods intertwined with sinewy muscle, like the skin has been pulled back to reveal the mechanics of his limbs. The artwork is intricate and beautiful. Makes me think of something broken that was fixed.

I suck in a breath when it hits me.

I know those arms, and I *know* those hands.

Chapter Seventeen

LEO

Skylar's been gone for three days. In the quiet of my own mind I admit to myself that I miss her.

Yes, I miss her because my daughter has been a restless and sometimes cranky disaster since she's been yanked out of her routine—that's part of it. Olivia is chomping at the bit to meet this baby, and I think she might even be a little jealous of James being that he's taken Skylar away from us—I mean her. But I also miss the warmth and fun she brings to our house. There are no dance-offs happening in the kitchen when I walk in the door from work, I burned the cheese on top of the chicken parm I attempted to cook on Sunday, and there's just a dullness that wasn't there before Skylar came onto the scene. She's spoiled us or ruined us. I'm not sure which.

I have to remind myself to turn on the music, to try to dance with Olivia and sing while we cook, but she isn't having it. My daughter loves me, I know that, but I also know I'm a piss poor substitute for the woman who has turned out to be our saving grace.

Her sister went a week past her due date before they induced the delivery, and the two women in this house were so keyed up in the days leading up to the birth that I felt like I was living through it with Garth and Sienna—two people I've never even met.

Skylar has been video chatting with Olivia every day, and I'm not sure if it's a good thing. My daughter practically rips the phone out of my hand when it rings at seven o'clock each night, desperate to see this girl who I hate to admit has become the primary female in her life.

A babysitter.

A college kid.

Olivia gets this wide-eyed, over the moon look on her face whenever she gets to see baby James. Skylar holds the phone close enough so that Olivia can hear him breathe in and out. He's so tiny, and seeing him brings me back to the days when I cradled my own little baby in my arms. I look on for a moment and then leave them to it. The sight of someone so small and helpless can flood me with love one moment and then a rush of painful memories the next.

I never asked, but always wondered why Carrie went ahead with the pregnancy. At first I just assumed that despite her faults, she believed that keeping the baby was just the morally right thing to do. So I figured Carrie would take to it—that once the baby was born she'd love it and hopefully change some of her own wild child ways. But Carrie didn't even want to hold Olivia in the hospital.

She looked beyond depressed, which scared the living hell out of me, and she didn't smile unless her friends came by the house with cute little baby gifts and bottles of prosecco to toast the new mom. She'd dress Olivia up on those days and put on a show, but behind closed doors when it was just us, she wouldn't get up off the couch even if Olivia was screaming bloody murder from her crib. Carrie would sit there like a stone, her face an impassive mask.

One night I broke down and shouted, "Just this once, could you get off your ass and check on your daughter?" because I'd basically been changing every diaper and doing every midnight feeding since I brought the two of them home from the hospital.

She looked to me, put her wineglass down and then leisurely made her way to the stairs. But I had to follow. I was already so attached to Olivia that I didn't trust Carrie around her. Didn't trust that she'd clean her thoroughly, didn't trust that she'd strap her onto the changing table, didn't trust her to do anything where my child was concerned.

She was never a warm and affectionate person, but I think having the baby broke something inside of Carrie. Maybe I should have moved us back to Cincinnati to be closer to her family like she asked. Maybe I should have made sure she had a good nanny to help her from day one. Maybe I should have pushed her to go to therapy sooner.

But I was twenty-five years old, not much more than a kid myself. I didn't know jack shit about postpartum depression, about marriage, about anything.

And it's hard to have sympathy for someone who started to run out on her kid any chance she could get. She was like a zombie when she was home with us, but when one of her old friends called with an invite for a girls' night out she morphed into her old party girl self.

She was back to her pre-pregnancy size within a month because she barely ate, so wine-soaked nights left her coming home in a taxi too drunk to exit the car without me and the driver having to carry her in. Not a good look. And, no surprise, Carrie would be useless the next day.

By the time Olivia was six months old I wanted out for me and my daughter. I'd stopped caring about my wife, figured that if she wanted to drink like a sorority girl and then lay around hungover all day, I could manage on my own because that's essentially what I was doing anyway.

My parents were too old to help in any real way, and Carrie's mom came to visit only once in the early days and was no help whatsoever.

Like mother like daughter, the only thing my mother-in-law did during her visit was to cheer her little girl up by taking her shopping all day, or to lunch and the spa on my dime. The two of them practically wore out the strip out on my credit card that week.

Carrie went home to Cinci when Olivia was around ten months old, and when she got back she sat me down with a look of cold determination. By then we were barely on speaking terms. It was like working an office job stuck in a cubicle next to that one coworker you just can't stand. She threw out the term *trial separation* but I knew she wanted a divorce. I wanted one too. But then she told me she was moving back home and taking Olivia with her.

I'd just secured my first really big patent the year before, and foolishly bragged to Carrie that the licensing deals alone would set me up with royalties for the rest of my days. Explaining the concept of mailbox money to her, I felt like a big shot, when in reality I was a colossal dumbass. Two months later I was married with a baby on the way, too shellshocked to even think of a pre-nup.

And that's how low my opinion of Carrie was at that

point. Custody of Olivia meant fat child support payments for my ex-wife. Clever girl would be getting her own mailbox money after all. I think I laughed in her face and said something original like: *Over my dead body.*

But it was her dead body I was standing over in the morgue only a few short weeks later. She died in a drunk driving accident. A passenger in some guy's car.

They left a club and were heading in the opposite direction of our house. After the accident one of her friends fessed up and confirmed what I already suspected. The man who survived the crash but would ultimately wind up serving two years for vehicular manslaughter was someone from Carries's past. Yeah, a real stand-up guy.

Hate is a strong word, but that's what I felt in the days and weeks leading up to her death. Hated her just as much or even more in the weeks and months that followed, as every new lie and deception came to light.

It's been over three years now, so I'm ashamed to admit there are times when I still hate her.

I hate that I have to speak about her in glowing terms to our daughter. Hate that I have to see her picture on Olivia's nightstand every time I tuck her in. Hate what she put me through, torturing me from beyond the grave when that piece of shit boyfriend of hers demanded a paternity test in a bid to garner some sympathy from the judge before he was sentenced.

Yeah, I still hate everything about Carrie except the miracle she gave to me.

Chapter Eighteen

SKYLAR

Sienna is folding some laundry, I think, and she's speaking to me but I'm finding it hard to listen.

Beautiful.

The word seems inadequate, but it's all I can think of when I look down into my nephew's face. His little body is so warm and soft, and it's as if he's nestled into my arms in a way that feels perfect—like God made babies to fit just so.

"He's perfect," I say to no one in particular.

Sienna stops what she's doing and sits at the foot of the bed where I'm lying. "I know. I feel like I spend most of the day just staring at him like you are now."

"I can't believe he's four weeks old already."

"Right? I feel like this month has flown by and I've barely left the house. You'd think I'd be stir crazy by now but I'm not."

"It'll be so nice when you can take him out for a walk."

Looking to the window, I shake my head. "It's April second and there's still snow on the ground."

"I'm not itching to be out and about just yet. It's been nice with just me and Garth and the baby holed up together. Grandy's visits make me want to tear my hair out sometimes, but she means well."

"I can't believe that nut chose to be called Grandy because it rhymes with her favorite cocktail."

We both laugh, but I seriously do think Garth's mom is a little touched in the head, and I'm not too keen on the idea of her caring for my little James.

"Aw, she's all right." I roll my eyes because my sister is just too damn nice sometimes. "I mean, she's not Mom, but she loves James more than anything. And I know I already thanked you for staying those first couple of days after I got home, but really, you were a lifesaver. I was a hormonal mess for a while there."

"Yeah, I miss Mom." I have to wipe at a stray tear when I look down at James sleeping peacefully. "She would have adored him."

"Dad, too."

I nod in agreement, still unable to talk about him in a positive way even though I can totally see my father sitting in his recliner with James in his arms, loving him as much as I do.

Sienna laughs. "Mom would absolutely freak if she saw the way Grandy burps James. I basically won't let her hold him after his feedings now because I'm afraid she'll give him shaken baby syndrome."

I can't help but laugh when Sienna puffs out her cheeks imitating her mother-in-law, pounding on her own chest like it's James's back.

"No making fun of my momma," Garth teases when he comes into the room.

"I love your mom, you know that. I just wish she wouldn't handle him the way she does. She's a tough old broad."

Garth lets out a loud, long belch himself and then says, "I turned out just fine."

I whisper, "Gross, Garth," because that disgusting noise has roused the baby.

Sienna muffles a laugh and whispers as she points to her husband, "I'm blaming Grandy and her violent burping methods for that."

"He's a man…Gotta learn to burp like a man."

I shake my head and smile. "I am sooo happy that I'm single right now."

Sienna settles in next to me and I hand James over when he opens his eyes. He usually wants some one-on-one time with my sister's boob as soon as he wakes up.

"Did he just smile at you?"

"Yes you did, didn't you?" Sienna coos as she gently rubs her finger across his chin.

"I mean, I've seen him do it before but that looked like a real genuine smile."

Garth says, "I think before it was just gas or something, but yeah, he smiles whenever he hears one of our voices now. Sienna more than me because, you know, she's got the milk." Moving in closer he whispers as he touches his hand to James's head. "I get it, little man. Mommy's got the best ta-tas in town."

I tease, "I'll take that as a compliment."

"As you should." He's still looking at his wife and child as he says it, and I find myself staring too as Sienna lifts her shirt and shifts the stretchy material of her nursing bra down. James latches onto her, taking long pulls and looking so very content.

I swallow to stem the tide of sadness that's taking hold. Why on earth am I sad? As much as I love James, I don't want a baby now. It's just human instinct, I tell myself. Ridiculous emotions stirred by evolution and Mother Nature herself. Shaking it off, I focus on mother and child again. It *is* amazing. It's like we women were made perfectly, with everything we need to nurture life just built right in.

"Amazing," I murmur.

"Amazing and hot as eff."

"As eff? Seriously? Do *not* be saying that kind of stuff around my nephew. He'll know what it means by the time he's two and you'll be getting him kicked out of preschool."

Garth raises his eyebrows in fear. "Point taken."

And at the mention of preschool, my mind goes back to Olivia. She's been itching to meet James, the poor little thing, but with the whole germ situation I know it's best to wait a few weeks.

"Are you sure it's all right to bring Olivia next week? I mean, I'll wash her hands like she's prepping for surgery and I'll cancel if she's so much as sniffling, but I'd totally understand if you don't want anyone unfamiliar around him yet."

Sienna has James on her shoulder, rubbing his back oh so gently when a burp comes out. "See?" She looks to Garth. "You get a nice, big burp from just *touching* this little guy's back."

"I'll tell Grandy but," he smiles, "you know she thinks she knows best."

"Knows best my ass...I mean butt," she whispers as James settles back into her arms and his eyes drift closed again.

"He sleeps, eats, pees and poops. I keep telling myself to enjoy the peace and quiet while it lasts but I love it when he stays awake for an hour or so." Garth takes him from Sienna and feels his diaper to make sure he's ok. "I'm gonna slip him into a dry one."

"Ok."

I shake my head even though I'm truly happy taking in my sister's dreamy expression. "Jeez, you still look at your husband that way?"

"She loves me, Sky. And who could blame her?"

"There is something undeniably sexy about a guy who changes diapers." Sienna turns back to me. "And yeah, you can definitely bring Olivia here. You talk about her so much that I'm kind of dying to meet her. And it's not like we've been in a total bubble. People have been popping in to see the baby."

"Yeah. My aunt and uncle were here last week, Sienna's boss and her husband came over for dinner one night, and Tyler's been by a few times."

"He's been here three separate times to be exact." Sienna adds, "I think he comes by hoping he'll run into you."

"How is he?"

Sienna looks to Garth before answering, "Good, I guess."

Garth says, "He's still with Lila, but that's a bit of a shit show."

"How so? I saw a few pictures on her profile," I feel my cheeks heat at the admission, "and they looked happy enough."

"You've looked her up?" Sienna seems genuinely surprised.

"I get bored sometimes. And I did date the boy for over two years. I mean, I still care about him."

"I don't like Lila for him," Garth says as he snaps James back into his onesie. "She can drink him under the table so she's not exactly encouraging him to stay on the straight and narrow."

"Yeah, I saw the picture she posted from Atlantic City on his birthday."

"And that was all her doing." Sienna shakes her head. "She surprised him with a road trip."

My heart is heavy when I snap, "No one forces him to gamble. That's on him. Just glad I don't have to play the role of nagging girlfriend anymore."

It's quiet for a minute before Garth says, "It's a shame, though. Lila's a good time girl, nothing more. She doesn't love him. No doubt she'll drop his ass when someone better comes along."

"Can you talk to him?" I ask Garth.

"He knows. And it's like you said, Tyler has to change. No one can do it for him."

Chapter Nineteen

LEO

Christ.

Olivia's been up since six this morning. She's so damn excited for today but the rain is coming down in sheets. No way am I letting the two of them drive an hour in this weather. And one look at the weather app on my phone shows there's no sign of this letting up.

Just as I'm about to text Skylar and tell her not to come, I hear a knock on the door followed by the excited squeal of a preschooler not a moment later.

Skylar is wearing a jacket that's doing a poor job of keeping her dry, with the wind whipping the hood back and off her head before she can get in the doorway.

"It's wicked out there!"

"I'm ready!" Olivia calls out, making her way down the stairs wearing the party dress my parents bought her for Christmas a few months ago. Totally impractical, she has nowhere to wear it, but Libs loves putting it on and dancing around in front of the mirror in her room.

Skylar says, "She's a trip," before turning her attention to Olivia. "Libby, *dah-ling*, you look fab!"

"Can I change James's diaper?"

"I don't see why not. I'll show you how. But maybe I'm going to pack you some comfy clothes to take along. You know, in case you want to play later on."

"Sky?" I gesture to the kitchen so we can speak privately. "The weather is pretty bad. I don't think—"

"Don't worry. I was totally going to stall until this lets up."

"It's not going to let up."

"Oh." She looks disappointed. "We can't go tomorrow... Garth's older brother is coming with his family." Turning to see Olivia coming into the kitchen wearing a frown, she says, "Maybe Tuesday? I could check with Sienna."

With that, Olivia collapses into a heap on the floor. I'd tag her as being melodramatic, except for the fact that she's shedding what looks like a bucketload of tears within a minute.

"No worries, Olivia." Skylar crouches down to her level. "It's just raining really hard out there. I promise we'll get there this week though, ok?"

That does nothing to cheer her up, so I join in and make it worse. "Olivia, crying and carrying on like this won't make me change my mind. It's not safe for Skylar to drive in this weather. You hear me?"

The wails just get louder and the tears don't stop. She actually says, "You're mean," before she starts hiccupping and making sounds like she's hyperventilating.

Skylar picks her up off the floor and takes her over to the couch, rubbing a hand over Olivia's back as she whispers soothing words into her hair.

I should be able to calm her down and take control of the situation, but looking over at the two of them, I decide that Skylar has a way better handle on this than I do at the moment. I'm not too proud to admit defeat. But it does worry me, this close attachment she has to Skylar. What happens when Skylar goes back home this summer? What happens if she doesn't come back to school in the fall? What if she finds another job?

I look out the window to see that the downpour has let up some, but if the weathermen are right then it's going to be raining off and on all day. I make a split-second decision before I can think it through. I was planning to get a ton of shit done today, but whatever.

"You can go, but only if I do the driving."

Olivia looks to me, wiping her eyes and still barely able to talk through her tears when she asks, "We can go?"

Her face is all blotchy and wet and her nose is running. Jesus, she must have been looking forward to this way more than I thought.

"If Skylar's all right with me driving you two."

"Of course I'm ok with it! I just don't want you giving up your day. I know you probably have work to do."

Olivia is already wiggling out of Skylar's lap and making her way to the stairs. "I be right back," she says.

"It's no big deal," I tell Skylar. "I'll bring my laptop and find a Starbucks. I can work anywhere."

"Well, there's no Starbucks but there is a diner about fifteen minutes from their place."

"No Starbucks?"

"Not one," she says laughing. "And if the diner isn't up to your standards then you're out of luck. The pizza shop doesn't have wi-fi and the sub shop doesn't have seats."

"I'll manage."

"Let me go up and help her wash her face. From the looks of the dress she picked out, Olivia's looking to make a good impression."

Ten minutes into the drive, I check the rearview mirror and see that Olivia is passed out cold. "I guess this morning's drama tired her out."

"I've never seen her like that. Minor meltdowns sure, but this morning was like...apocalyptic."

I nod my head and smile, relieved that it's behind us. "Apocalyptic is a good word. I like that one." Skylar turns to look at me a moment later when I say, "She's very attached to you."

She sees the worry on my face and shoots me a soft smile. "That's a good thing. Healthy attachments are necessary for us primates. And that's not just my opinion, that comes courtesy of every expert on developmental theory from Darwin to Piaget."

I lower my head and nod, embarrassed for some reason.

"I feel sort of responsible for this morning. I've just been so excited about James. Maybe me talking about him all the time and showing her pictures hyped this visit up too much."

"Don't go taking credit for her temper tantrum. I'm not and I'm the one who started her off. That was one hundred percent Libs. And you *should* be hyped up about becoming an aunt for the first time. A new baby in the family changes everything. Holding a baby for the first time..."

She picks up where I trail off. "Oh, I wasn't ready for it. You think Olivia was bawling back there? I spouted like a faucet the first time I held James in my arms."

"I think I was speechless for a full five minutes when I first held Olivia."

"Aw, so under that grumpy exterior you're really just a mush like me. I knew it."

"Grumpy? That's how you see me?"

"Well, you made some first impression when you barged into the office that day."

My eyes go wide. "Are you serious? I was worried out of my mind."

"And that help wanted ad? Brutal."

"Direct and to the point is the way I'd describe it."

She laughs and nudges my knee with her hand. "I was scared out of my mind walking into your house that first time. I was expecting you to blow a whistle like that father in *The Sound of Music*...Captain Von Trapp."

"Never saw it."

"Yeah," she smiles my way and teases, "I don't suppose you'd like it. Might hit too close to home."

"Jeez...Who knew you were such a wiseass." I don't say it with a smile but I am smiling on the inside. I don't get much of a chance to talk one-on-one with Skylar, and I'm liking this relaxed and playful side of her.

She rests her head back against the seat. "I had a rough couple of months there, but I finally feel like I'm getting back to my old self."

"And your old self was a wiseass?"

"Sometimes." She looks back to make sure Olivia is still asleep. "But I meant that I finally feel like I've found my footing again. I feel more confident and I'm happy most of the time...More like I used to be. Leaving home to come to school was harder than I'd anticipated."

I wrestle with whether or not to go there for a moment,

but she's opening up to me and the temptation to know more about her is too strong. "You suffered a tremendous loss, too. I'm impressed that you even had it in you to tackle college after what you went through."

"Don't be impressed. College was my way to escape from all that hurt. I got a perfect GPA for the fall semester because I was basically running on auto-pilot."

"I call bullshit." She looks to me, her eyes wide in surprise. "I mean, you're completely engaged when you're with my daughter. I see it. I'd never in a million years describe you as running on auto-pilot."

Skylar turns and smiles at Olivia's sleeping face. "I think she kind of saved me these past few months. It's hard to wallow in grief when you've got someone depending on you."

"I can relate to that."

She clears her throat before asking, "Feel free to tell me to can it if this is too personal, but how old was Olivia when her mother died?"

"It was just before her first birthday. She, uh, her mother died in a car accident."

I hear her breath catch. "Leo, I'm so sorry."

"Thank you."

"No...I mean, yes, I am sorry for your loss, but I'm sorry about today. And I'm sorry about making fun of your want ad. You must be worried anytime Olivia gets into a car with anyone but you."

"I wouldn't have let you two drive today even if that never happened."

"But still, I should have been more sensitive."

"No way you could have known."

After a moment of silence that for some reason doesn't feel

one bit uncomfortable, she says, "She asks about her. More frequently these past few weeks."

"Think maybe all the baby James talk has something to do with it?"

"Probably. But I also think it has to do with school."

"How so?"

"I watch her at pick-up time. She looks for me and smiles when she's running towards me, but in those few seconds before she spots me, sometimes I see her focusing in on the other kids. There aren't a lot of other babysitters picking up. A few fathers, but it's mainly moms."

"Yeah, I've noticed that too."

She nods her head knowingly when she says, "I'm sure you have."

I don't get it, and tell her just that.

"Let's just say a few of them look *very* disappointed when I get out of the car. I think you've got a few fan club members."

"What?"

Now she's full on belly laughing. "There's one, little Sarah's mom? She asks about you all the time. It's like she's a CIA agent digging for intel." In a more quiet voice she adds, "I think she kind of hates me because I basically answer *I don't know* to every question. And really, I *don't* know."

"What does she ask?"

"Oh, she's just a pain. She asks about Olivia's mother." Skylar pretends she's sucking on a vape pen and switches over to an annoying, nasally voice. "What's the story there? Like, is he single?" Looking to me, she adds, "Mind you, she is *not* single from what I've gathered, so her interest in you makes her all the more heinous."

"How do you answer her?"

"It's not just her that I have to contend with. I'd say there are three or four thirsty ladies in total. And I don't tell them squat." She looks mildly offended. "I'd never."

"There's really nothing to tell."

She looks away, gazes out the passenger side window. "I don't know about that. I'd say you're a pretty interesting person."

"Are we there yet?" a groggy voice calls from the back seat.

Skylar looks at her phone. "Ten minutes, angel."

"You got my cup?"

"Of course, mademoiselle," Skylar answers as she rummages through her bag.

"Olivia, maybe instead you could try saying something like, 'Skylar, may I please have my cup?'" And for some reason they both find that very entertaining. "What? Is it wrong to start teaching her better manners?"

Olivia ignores me, taking the cup from Skylar and slurping the contents down, while Skylar is still wearing a teasing smile. "That's what I'm talking about. That was a total Captain Von Trapp move."

She smiles all the time, but for some reason it feels different today. Maybe it's because we're sitting side by side talking in a way that's more personal than we have before, maybe it's because her smiles are directed at me and no one else. Whatever the reason, it's affecting me more than it should. I like this connection, this warmth and familiarity—I like seeing her happy. Doesn't matter that she's only smiling because she's making fun of me. Let her. Even when she teases it's good natured. I just don't think she has it in her to be unkind.

I find that I'm smiling when I look away from her and back to the road. "We might have to schedule a movie night."

"Totally! Olivia's seen it before. She loves it."

"Love what?"

"I was just telling your dad that we love *The Sound of Music*. He wants to watch it with us one day."

In the rearview mirror I see Olivia's eyes light up when she says, "Yes!" But then she breaks out into song, and I've never been so happy to see that the GPS now reads only three minutes to our destination.

"I am sixteen, uh, uh, seventeen," she belts out.

"See," Skylar's grinning from ear to ear, "it's educational too. Olivia can count to twenty because of that movie."

"Twenty? Hah, she already knew how to do that. Nice try, Obi-Wan."

"Obi-Wan? How very predictable, the engineer is a Star Wars geek. And I'm sure you already know this, but naming numbers to twenty is vastly different from pairing the appropriate number of objects with a number. From one geek to another, *I'm* the one who taught her that."

"A geek, huh? Bet a certain someone's mother wouldn't call me that," I tease, referring to our conversation from before.

"No, she probably wouldn't." She shakes her head. "Please swear to me upon pain of death that you won't ever talk to her, let alone date her. You should hear the way she snaps at," she moves her lips to form the girl's name silently. "She's not a good person." When I don't respond she turns to me with a worried look. "Sorry, I shouldn't have brought up the d-a-t-e thing."

"D-a-t-e. Date!" Olivia exclaims.

As we pull up in front of the address, Skylar answers my shocked expression. "Yeah, her reading skills are going through the roof. She's like a sponge." Turning to Olivia, she high-fives her and says, "Way to work that silent E!"

I drive off after Skylar gives me the name of the diner and I see a younger guy, early twenties, walk outside and wave to Skylar as she's getting Olivia out of her seat.

She asked me to come inside but I made up an excuse. Just felt like I'd be barging in on her life without really being invited. Today was supposed to be about Olivia meeting her family. I was just a last-minute, unexpected addition to this outing.

I drive back to the main street, thinking there must be somewhere closer than the diner one town over. It's nothing like what I expected. Skylar mentioned once before that she grew up in a small town, but this is more than small, it's desolate. Main Street has more shuttered store fronts than open businesses, and most of the homes I pass aren't well maintained.

I make it to the diner and settle in at a corner booth. I power up my laptop, order some coffee and an egg sandwich, but I'm useless as far as getting work done goes. I have this heavy weight on me, a sorrow that I can't immediately define. But it doesn't take much soul searching to know that it's Skylar who has me feeling this way.

I knew she had it hard, what with losing her parents so young and the circumstances surrounding their death, but seeing first-hand where she comes from has me feeling her pain as if it's my own.

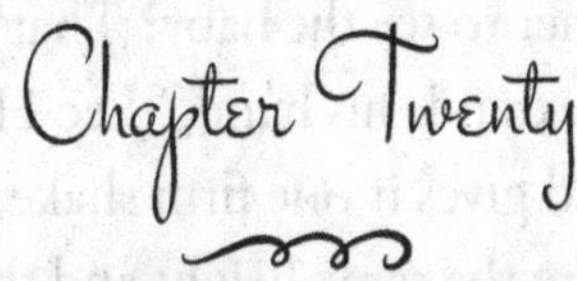

SKYLAR

"Whose rich prick-mobile is parked out front?"

Ah, he always did know how to make an entrance.

My cheeks flush as I look to Leo, whose brows are creased as he takes in Tyler, the guy who just introduced his daughter to a fabulous new word.

"Come on in, Tyler," Garth says as he gets up from the table, shooting me a nervous look in the process.

I stay in my seat but feel as jumpy as a jack rabbit. "Hi, Tyler."

"Hey, Sky." He looks around, pauses when he sets his eyes on Olivia sitting on the floor next to James's little cushioned mat, and then again when he looks at Leo sitting next to me at the table. "How are you?" he asks once he finishes taking an inventory of the room.

"I'm good, how about you?"

"Same...You know," he answers absently.

"Tyler, that's Olivia over there with James, and this is her father, Leo. I, um, work for them. I mean, uh, I'm Olivia's babysitter."

Fixing his eyes on Leo he says, "And you made the trip down here all together to see the baby? That's nice."

Leo stands and extends his hand. "Leo Hale."

Tyler takes it and gives it one firm shake, sizing Leo up as if they're rivals. They're the same height and their builds are similar, but they are no match. Leo exudes power, along with an air of confidence that's hard for someone in Tyler's state to come by.

Leo's probably having a laugh at Tyler and his juvenile show of jealousy right now, even though he's doing an admirable job of hiding it. And all the while I sit like a stone, paralyzed by my discomfort.

Sienna makes her way over to Tyler and gives him the hug that I should be offering. "Sit down, Tyler. I'll make you a plate."

"No, thanks." He pats his middle. "Just ate."

Leo shifts his chair back and stands up again. Looking to me he says, "I'll start getting Olivia ready to go and meet you out in the car...No rush." He looks to Sienna and Garth. "It was nice to meet you both, and congratulations on James again. And thank you for lunch, Sienna. It was great."

"Anytime. And I should be thanking you...I think I may have found myself a new babysitter." Reaching down to lift the baby, Sienna says, "Olivia, I'm so happy you came and helped us with James today. He's about to go down for his nap now. Can you bring the little lion you got for him? I think he'd like you to put that with the other toys in his room."

Sienna's good. She's got those diversion tactics down to a

science already. Instead of protesting, Olivia hops up and follows my sister inside with the stuffed animal and then comes back out smiling a minute later. "James is taking a nap."

Leo has gone out to the car with Olivia's dress and sparkly shoes while I busy myself gathering up the rest of our things. Garth takes two beers out of the fridge and hands one to Tyler.

"Libs, let's take our stuff out to the car." I look back to the guys. "Tell Sienna I'll be right back."

It takes just a few steps to get to the car, but in that short time I get soaked because I'm using my coat to shield Olivia. The rain has picked up again and the cold, biting wind seems fitting. I can't even look at Leo as I strap Olivia in. "Be back in a second, ok?"

"Take your time," he answers.

Tyler is waiting for me when I come back inside shivering and Garth has disappeared.

"Can we talk for a minute, Sky?"

"Sure, and I'm...I'm sorry that was so weird before." I peel off my sweater and throw a spare flannel over my damp t-shirt. "I wasn't expecting you."

He lets out a sad laugh. "I keep coming by hoping to catch you but my timing has been for shit lately." He shakes his head and then fixes his sad eyes on mine. "Are you with him?"

"No! He's my boss, that's it. He just drove today because Olivia was looking forward to it and the weather was terrible. No...Leo? No."

I want to suck the words back in as I'm spitting them out, knowing I doth protest way, way, *way* too much. In a desperate effort to change the subject, I turn the tables on him. "Are you still with Lila?"

"I've never been *with* her, Sky. Never the way I was with

you. If I thought for one second I had a chance with you then I'd never set eyes on her or anyone else again. You know that, don't you?"

I want to turn to sand, to disintegrate and blow away. I can't face him, can't bring myself to hurt him more than I already have. "I'm sorry," is all I can manage. "I'm sorry, Tyler."

I don't look up, so I don't see him make his way to the door. I only hear the howling wind and the rain as it pelts against the trailer's aluminum siding. Sienna and Garth come back into the main room to find me shaking.

"Oh, Sky," my sister says as she wraps me in her arms. "Are you all right?"

"I'm fine. That was just…" I take a deep breath. "I'll call you tonight. I don't want to leave them waiting too long."

I give Garth a quick hug and then run back outside into the rain.

"Are you good?" he asks as he takes me in and then turns the heat up high.

"Yeah, I'm ready to go."

We drive the first half hour in silence. Olivia is awake for the first fifteen minutes or so, and then I look back to see her heavy lids closing. Leo keeps his eyes fixed straight ahead and I'm grateful for it. I don't want to face him just yet.

Nothing really happened, I tell myself. There was no show down, no drama. When I texted Leo and told him to come for lunch he declined at first, texting back that he didn't want to intrude on my family time. But then he relented when I told him Sienna and Garth wanted to meet him and that she'd made her famous fish tacos, a dish he'd regret missing out on. It was casual and easy at the table with them. I was relaxed and happy. But now I feel exposed for some reason. I'm embarrassed.

"I take it that guy is your boyfriend or he was at some

point?" He looks to me before setting his eyes back on the road. Echoing my words from before, he adds, "You can tell me to can it if you don't want to talk about it."

I don't want to talk about it, but at the same time I do. It's stupid, this need I have to clarify that I am, in fact, unattached. It's not like Leo cares. He has no memory whatsoever of that night. I'm sure of it.

"We broke up a few weeks after my parents died."

"He doesn't seem like he's taking it all that well."

"You got that from what? From that minute-long exchange?"

"Do you think it's so hard to read people? To read men?"

"I don't know what I think." I trace my finger along the window, writing my name in the fogged-up glass. "I just know that he's a good person and I've hurt him."

"You don't seem like the kind of person who goes around intentionally hurting people. Just sayin'..."

"Sometimes it's just inevitable. The only thing that would make Ty happy is the two of us getting back together again, and that will never happen."

"Never is a strong word. What if you were trapped on a deserted island with no chance of rescue?"

I picture Lila sauntering out of his bedroom practically naked. "Never."

Leo keeps his eyes trained on the road. "Zombie apocalypse and he's your only shot at survival?"

I don't miss a beat. "Nope, not happening."

"What if he swore on his life that he'd never *ever* do the thing that made you break it off with him in the first place?"

I picture Tyler watching a football game, cursing at the television screen when the field goal kick doesn't go his way. "That's a promise he can't keep."

I fix my eyes on the scenery outside and that's when I notice that the rain has turned heavy and wet. Leo turns on the news radio channel just in time to hear the announcer forecast snow squalls and possible accumulation for tonight.

"You gotta love springtime in Pennsylvania."

"I'll take you straight back to your dorm."

"That's out of the way. Get Olivia home and then I'll head back when there's a break in the weather."

"No. I don't want you driving in this."

"But I'm picking Olivia up from school on Monday, remember?"

"Yeah...Maybe we can switch it up next week? I'll cover Monday and then we can do a full day on Tuesday? But only if it works for you."

"That works."

"Good. Oh, and you just reminded me...There's a race in Miami in two weeks and the team sponsor really wants me to attend. It's the biggest race second only to Daytona and I've backed out on the last few events. It would be for an entire weekend, though. Are you up for that?"

"I'm up for it, but is it the weekend of the twenty-first?"

"I think so. You're not available? It's fine if you can't do it."

"What would you do, have Maureen cover it?"

I know Leo still asks her to fill in when he's desperate, but leave Olivia in Maureen's care for an entire weekend?

His brow furrows as if he's thinking the same exact thing. "I'll figure something out."

"I promised Garth and Sienna I'd watch James that weekend, but I might have a solution. They never had a real honeymoon when they got married, and Garth was able to borrow a friend's cabin *and* get some time off, so I don't want to disappoint them. I was planning to head down there Friday night after you get home, but if I watch James at your house then I can get him Friday morning and be back in time to get Olivia from school. I think she'd be on board with that plan."

We both laugh when Leo shoots back, "You *think* she'd be on board?" but then he shakes his head. "I can't ask you to do that. Sounds like a lot of work."

"It might work out even better. The cabin is up in Erie. They'll be passing right through here on their way home. Actually, I won't even have to drive down to get him. They can just drop James off with us on Saturday morning."

He comes to a stop outside of my dorm. "If you're sure it's all right. I mean, I'd much rather leave Olivia with you."

And that right there? His trust, knowing he appreciates the job I'm doing with his daughter—I must be an emotional mess today because those words leave me on the verge of teary-eyed.

"Great. It's settled then." I look behind me to see that Olivia's still out cold. "Late afternoon nap. Good luck getting her to sleep tonight."

He pretends to be offended. "You think I don't have any tricks up my sleeve? She'll be tucked in by eight."

I roll my eyes. "She told me she watched the *American Idol* finale with you last week. I know for a fact that didn't end until eleven."

"Whatever. At least it wasn't *The Bachelor.* Maureen would have had that cued up for the two of them to watch together."

I'm standing outside now, leaning down to speak to him through my door that's still open. "You're exaggerating. I love that lady. She's a spitfire."

"A spitfire. Is that a nice way of saying she's a hellion who won't listen to anyone?"

He's smiling and I'm enjoying this easy back and forth between us way too much.

"Hey," he looks past me, "I think someone is waiting on you."

I turn to see a bundled-up Pilar waving to me from just few feet away. "Sky, I thought that was you."

Looking back to Leo, I do my best to smile through my disappointment. "Thanks for the ride. I'll see you Tuesday at around ten-thirty?"

"See you then." As I turn to go he calls after me, "And thanks for today. I'm glad I got to meet your family. They're great."

I nod, fighting back the flood of emotion brought on by the reminder of family. There's gratitude and grief associated with the word.

"Hey, girl." Pilar greets me with a smile and a hug. And it's good when she pulls me in close. The contact is something I desperately need at the moment and it gives me the additional few seconds I need to compose myself.

"What are you doing all the way over here on this side of campus?"

"A friend of mine, Ghislaine, lives here. She's a French Literature major. Do you know her?"

"Is she an international student?"

"Yes." Pilar smirks. "She's from Lyon."

"I'd say she took the easy way out with that major but plenty of native English speakers major in English Lit."

"Good point." Pilar shivers as I fiddle with my key card. "But she'll freely admit to taking the easy way out."

"I haven't met her. I'd remember that name. Do you only associate with glamorous people who have international jet-setter type names?"

"Mais non, Skylar! I *do* hang out with you." She pairs that dig with a hip check.

Climbing the stairs, she asks, "What's the story with that guy who dropped you off?"

I turn back with a raised eyebrow. "The story?"

"Isn't he that guy…The one who…I know I heard him speak at some professional development lecture series last year. It was on patent acquisition." She's laughing when she says, "I remember sitting there lost in a fantasy of that man mauling me in some dark empty classroom. Everyone said it was really informative but I barely heard a word he said."

"You're an engineering major?"

"Mathematics."

"That's what I thought."

"I was just tagging along that day with Devon. So what's the story?"

"No story. I babysit for his daughter. His name is Leo Hale. And he probably was the speaker. I know he does something with patents and he's involved with the engineering department's research in some way."

"Leo Hale…Yeah. Devon was saying he secured his first patent for some polymer-based sealant used in auto manufacturing *before* he finished his undergrad."

"Wow." I try to play down my reaction and come off as neutral. "That's impressive."

"He looks like a hot lumberjack. Mmm…So much intelligence packed into that manly man." We're standing at the other end of my hallway. "What's he like?" she asks, and I think on that loaded question as she's knocking on her friend's door.

"He's just a good person."

She introduces me to her friend and then kisses me goodbye on both cheeks because that's what the Pilars, Simones and Ghislaines of this world do. Even if they are from Cleveland, like Simone.

"I'll see you Thursday."

"We're hitting that new beer garden in Troy Hill." I turn back and nod, agreeable but noncommittal. Her smile tells me she knows I'm not coming but she'll give me a hard time about it anyway. She calls after me, "Just two more weeks until the recital," and just the reminder of it has me quaking in fear.

It's actually less than two weeks away. It's a week from this Thursday. And I'm doing a contemporary duet with Misha, so I'm kind of freaking out. At the holiday recital I was hidden in the background, no pressure at all. And while Misha's doing all of the heavy lifting in this piece he choreographed himself— I'm literally following his lead—I'll still be dancing center stage and I don't think I'm ready for prime time.

Grace is coming. She bawled me out over text message last week when she found out about the recital on her own. I was going to tell her, swear to God, but inviting people or announcing it in any way makes it real and scares me half to death. Sienna knows about it but she's not coming up. I patently forbid her to come. She's nursing, the baby can't sit through a show like that, and she has to get ready for their belated honeymoon getaway weekend.

That reminds me that I have to call my sister and tell her about the change in plans and make sure she's all right with it. It also reminds me that I have a crap ton of work to get done in the next week. There's only one month left in the semester so finals will be coming up before I know it. I can't lose focus because I cannot lose my scholarship. Dip below a three-five and I'll be out on my behind.

It's cumulative, I tell myself. And I kicked ass last semester so I don't have much to worry about. Tossing my bag onto my bed, I continue the positive self-talk, smiling to myself remembering the high school guidance counselor who taught me this technique. State what you're afraid of and then take a realistic inventory of whether or not the fear is warranted.

Feeling more relaxed and composed a few minutes later, I power up my laptop and get to work on a paper that's not due for two weeks. Tackle the obstacles in your path one by one.

Ah, Mr. Vargas.

If he only knew the number of times I've repeated his pearls of wisdom like a mantra to get me through this past year. Without knowing it he helped me untangle the mess my parents left behind, guided me through my breakup with Tyler, and strengthened my resolve whenever my lonely heart wavered.

And then there's Grace. She helped me stay the course when I questioned whether or not I belonged here, and she pushed me to step out of my comfort zone and try something new and scary.

Yeah, I'm still scared about being up on that stage, but thinking more rationally now, I know I'll get through it.

I've been fortunate to have people in my life who've encouraged me and gotten me through hard times, but Sienna trumps them all. She will always be my biggest cheerleader. Her voice is always in my head, coming in clearer and louder than the rest, and she's telling me I can do this, piece of cake.

I laugh when I can hear her imitating that character in *The Help*. It's her favorite book. *Yes*, I tell myself, *I'm smart, I'm important*. But Sienna never says it as a joke. She wants me to believe it about myself. She is the kindest person I know, and in some ways, the wisest. Sienna inherited all of my mother's best qualities and, I'll admit begrudgingly, my father's.

I think back to what Leo said before about my family. *They're great*. I wipe at the tears forming, try to stop the tide, but then I lie back on my bed and let it wash over me.

They were flawed but my parents *were* great. And the family I have left, Sienna, Garth and James? Great doesn't even do them justice.

So I'll add one more thing to those lines Sienna recites so often: *I am blessed*.

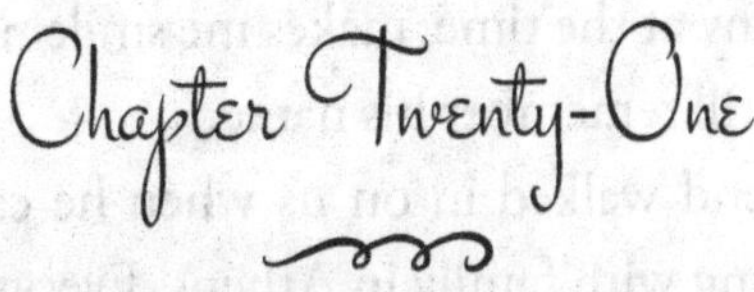

Chapter Twenty-One

LEO

I hate traveling.

I used to love it. Used to love seeing new cities, eating foods that were exotic and unfamiliar. I used to love adventure.

Sitting in my roomy first-class seat that still manages to feel cramped and uncomfortable, my mind goes back to a summer spent backpacking through Europe. Beer and wine-soaked nights in too many places to name.

I smile thinking back to the two weeks I spent in Santorini. Eleni...I thought I was in love with her without even knowing what the word meant.

Her English wasn't so hot and I spoke virtually no Greek, so our love affair wasn't exactly based on some deep mutual admiration or anything resembling it.

For two weeks I ate at the beachside café where she worked, waiting for her shift to end so that we could spend every night together. I entertained fantasies of bringing her home with me, as if a place like Pittsburgh was someplace to lure a beautiful twenty-year-old who already resided in paradise.

My seat mate looks my way when I laugh so I school my expression, but the memory of that morning, while it was the opposite of funny at the time, makes me smile now.

Giorgos. I still remember his name.

Her boyfriend walked in on us when he came back a day early from visiting with family in Athens. Everything is a blur, a frenzied, chaotic mess. Same as it was that morning. White sheets flying and twisting, heated words I didn't understand, a fully-clothed guy fighting me to the death as I hit back hard, bare-assed and confused.

I moved on to the next place with my buddies. I think it was Seville. I licked my wounds for a few days and then got back in the game. I was a ladies man that summer—never was before and haven't been since. I had a good run, I guess, but I'm not cut out for that kind of drama.

I came back after that summer, started graduate school and started my business. Got serious, as they say.

I was serious about Carrie in the beginning, probably because I was so distracted. But it took less than a year for me to know she was not the one.

I raise my hand to get the flight attendant's attention and then order a scotch and soda. I don't normally drink during flights because it makes me feel like crap, but thinking about Carrie sucks the life out of me. I need something to help me forget.

I try to go back to Eleni, but the face that's gone hazy in my memory suddenly morphs into Skylar's. I don't fight it or scold myself like I usually do. No, I let her in and let myself focus on the things in this world that are good and beautiful. Settling back into my seat, I take a sip and think of her without guilt, and without one ounce of self-restraint.

She blew me away last night.

Sky didn't tell us about the recital. I only found out when I ran into her friend Grace when I was leaving campus one afternoon. I didn't even question my decision to surprise her, told myself I was doing this for Olivia and no one else.

Yeah, right.

I didn't spring it on Olivia until a few hours before the show when I stopped at a flower shop after picking her up from school. Libby was so excited picking out the bouquet for Skylar, and then she dressed up like she was going to opening night at Lincoln Center, complete with her Dorothy-inspired sparkly red shoes.

We got two seats around ten rows back from the stage. I had to remind Olivia that she couldn't call out to Skylar, and raised up a silent thank you when she complied. I think for the first time in her life, Olivia was speechless, her eyes glued to the stage once the curtain came up and she spotted Skylar dancing back-up in the chorus. I'm sure the lead soloist was talented, but I didn't look at her once. My eyes were trained on Skylar's every move too.

And nothing could have prepared me for the second to last dance on the program. I looked down to see Olivia's eyes go wide when Skylar took the stage with just one other person.

With her hair tied up like that, she looked poised. She was an entirely different version of the girl who dances around my kitchen in jeans, laughing and singing, hair down and untamed. Dressed in only a black leotard, every curve of Skylar's body was on display. Every muscle in her slender arms, and in the strong legs that supported her through every graceful turn, spin and jump.

Her partner's presence barely registered. It seemed like he was there just to highlight her beauty. But in the closing moments of the number, when she laid on the stage and he raised himself above her in a handstand, their eyes fixed on one another, then I took notice.

I cannot fathom the level of strength and control it took to lower himself down the way he did, slow and curving his body with the flexibility of a cobra. He made contact with her chin to chin, chest to chest, then hip to hip, until they were connected from head to toe and he moved with her in a way that wasn't overtly sexual, but it was. And the way she moved with him left my throat dry. No different from a man crawling through the desert desperate for water.

I didn't even watch when the next dancer took the stage for the final performance. Didn't come back to my senses until the curtain lifted again and the crowd began clapping and getting up to give the troupe a well-deserved standing ovation.

I lifted Olivia up so she could see over the adults, and saw Skylar's teary-eyed smile when she caught sight of Olivia waving frantically.

Olivia didn't stop clapping until long after the curtain came down and just about everyone else cleared out of the aisles around us.

"The tulips, Daddy!"

I reached down to where I'd carefully placed the bouquet under my seat. "I don't know how this works, baby girl. We might have to save these until tomorrow."

"No." She fixed me with the most earnest expression. "I have to see her now."

And right on cue, Skylar and some of the other dancers came back out to see the few friends and family members who lingered.

Skylar made her way over with her dance partner and another performer. "This is the best surprise ever!" She wrapped her arms around Olivia and then looked back up to her friends. "Pilar, Misha...This is my Olivia. And this is Leo, her father."

I take another sip and replay the way she said it: *my Olivia*. Maybe the scotch is responsible for mellowing me out, but I come to the conclusion that I like it. I like the way Skylar makes my daughter feel singled-out and special.

Olivia. I shake my head at that kid's sometimes awkward, sometimes impeccable timing. Just as I was about to say my hellos and compliment them on the show, Olivia poked Skylar's dance partner in the side and said, "Are you Skylar's boyfriend?"

"Olivia!" Shaking my head in embarrassment, I looked to the guy Misha and apologized on behalf of my big-mouthed daughter even though I was secretly glad she'd asked. I was curious to know the answer to that question myself.

Skylar's cheeks turned red as her friends busted out laughing. Misha said, "No, sweetie. She's gorgeous and she danced like a star tonight, but sadly, she's just not my type."

Olivia answered with a simple, *oh*, obviously confused.

And I hate to admit it, but his answer made my night.

I cleared my throat and handed her the flowers. "These are for you." Looking to her friends to mask my own discomfort, I added, "You were all amazing. It was a great show."

Skylar crouched down. "Did you like it, Libs?"

Olivia answered her while twirling in a circle, "I loved it!"

When Grace came over with her man and hugged Sky, I decided we should go. I was feeling things that weren't necessarily new when it came to Skylar, but the force of my emotions were something new and confusing, and it felt wrong.

Sucking the last drop from my glass, I signal the flight attendant for another drink.

She'll never be *my* Skylar.

It can't happen.

I need to forget about her, too.

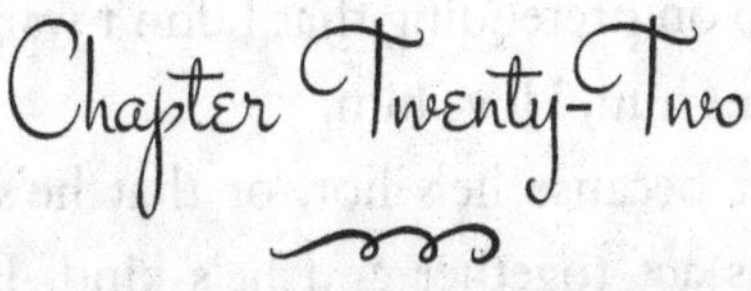

Chapter Twenty-Two

SKYLAR

The weekend started out great.

I was riding high after our show Thursday night. I even caved in and went out dancing with my friends at some new club downtown. I skipped the martinis this time, though. I didn't need the liquid courage and I was practically walking on air after killing it with Misha in our duet.

When I first saw Olivia and Leo in the crowd, I was beyond shocked. I never breathed a word of it to Olivia, knowing she'd hound her dad about coming. And I would never in a million years have invited Leo. I was so damn nervous before the show that it took me no less than five attempts to fasten my bra before I was successful. The thought of him watching me up there would have totally messed with my focus.

So it was a good thing I didn't spot them until the curtain call. And then I was glad he came, not to mention a little bit emotional about it. It was a sweet thing to do for his little girl, but maybe it meant more. Things had changed between us since our road trip to my hometown. It was subtle—and who knows, maybe I was totally imagining it—but he was looking at me differently, studying me in a way that gave me a ridiculous sense of hope.

I've given up on pretending that I don't want him. I dream about him, I want him, I love him.

And it's not because he's hot, or that he's intelligent, or that he's got his act together and he's kind. It's all of those things and so much more. When I see the way he interacts with Olivia, I can't imagine there's a man on the planet more caring and devoted than he is. I want to know what it feels like to have the love of a man like Leo Hale.

I was still riding high on Friday afternoon when I picked up a very excited Olivia from school and then raced back to the house to meet Sienna and Garth. Once they heard Leo was leaving Friday morning, they asked if they could tack an extra night onto their trip. Two nights? Sure. Piece of cake.

Not.

James is beyond adorable and I love, love, love him—don't get me wrong—but he does *not* willingly take a bottle, as promised, and he doesn't sleep anywhere *close* to four hours straight, as those two con artists led me to believe.

Last night was rough. James was up half the night and then *finally* went down for a snooze at six a.m. but Olivia woke up half an hour later, bright-eyed, bushy-tailed and ready to play with the baby. I put on a cartoon, begged her not to wake him and then nodded off with her on my lap, figuring that if she made a move I'd wake up. And it worked, I think.

I had big plans for Saturday, now that the weather finally got the memo that it was late April, but alas, we never made it out of the house. Between changing diapers, entertaining Olivia, and cleaning spit-up off the couch, my clothes, and the carpet because he did *not* like the baby formula or the breast milk Sienna pumped in advance—let's just say I was dragging ass by noon.

By six o'clock I was back in my pajama shorts, wearing my one and only clean shirt while the rest of my clothes were in the washing machine. Olivia and I had chocolate chip cookies for dinner, washed down with orange juice, and the poor thing was wiped out and in bed by eight-thirty after dancing and singing her little head off all day in an effort to entertain a very cranky James.

I'm not expecting anyone, so I should be mildly alarmed when I hear the front door open a few hours later, but I've just got no gas left in the tank.

I turn to see Leo surveying the disaster that was once his clean house. There are toys all over the living room, the sink is filled with dishes, and I probably look like I just went nine rounds with Rhonda Rousey.

"Hi," I whisper from the couch.

"Hey." He looks like he's trying not to smile. "Rough night?"

"Not too bad."

"Yeah?" He lets out a soft laugh. "Is he colicky or something?"

"He never was before. It's like he won't take the bottle from me for some reason."

"And he usually takes one no problem?"

"I've seen Garth feed him a bottle and he guzzles it right down. Grandy, that's Garth's mother...her too. He's just been so fussy. I've never seen him like this before."

He pulls his collar away from his neck like he's overheated or something. "I'm gonna go out on a limb here and guess that your sister is breast feeding him?"

I nod and then follow the path Leo's eyes are taking. James is squirming around again, his mouth making an eager attempt to get at my boob. Great. I'm too tired to do anything but throw my head back in exhaustion.

"Poor little guy is just confused. You look just like his momma. Probably smell just like her too." He comes closer and leans in to take him from me. "Can I give it a try?"

"Have at it."

James looks like a peanut in Leo's arms. He settles the two of them into the recliner, tests a drop of the warmed breastmilk on the inside of his wrist, and then eases the nipple into James's mouth. I'm so tired I can barely focus, but I do see that James is looking up at Leo wide-eyed as he slurps the contents of the bottle down.

"That's a good boy," Leo whispers to James. "Yeah, you were starving little man, weren't you?"

"Hey, what are you doing home?"

"Race was over," he says in a hushed tone. "I did my corporate duty. I'm all for networking, but not so much for the glad-handing, ass-kissing BS that was going on down there." He shifts James to lay on his chest and then rubs circles onto his back the same gentle way Sienna does it. His hand spans the width of James's back, and no more than five seconds pass before Leo is rewarded with a big burp. "Best sound ever."

I use every ounce of energy I have left to stand. "I'll take him now. I should change his diaper before he nods off again."

Leo shakes his head. "Just get the diaper bag for me. I want you to get some rest. I'll change him and then finish this bottle off so he's got a nice full belly."

"I can't let you do that. You must be tired after your trip."

He gestures to where I've set up a pillow and blanket on the couch. "You lay down. I'm not tired. And I'm kind of loving this stroll down memory lane." Breathing James in, he adds, "I haven't held a baby in a long time."

And I can see from the look on his face that he means it. Leo looks content. And even in this near-comatose state I'm in, I fight to keep my eyes open, transfixed by the sight of him cradling my nephew in his strong arms.

Fatherhood is sexy.

One last time I ask him, "Are you sure?"

"Hundred percent. Now lay down and get some rest."

Part Three

BECAUSE THE NIGHT

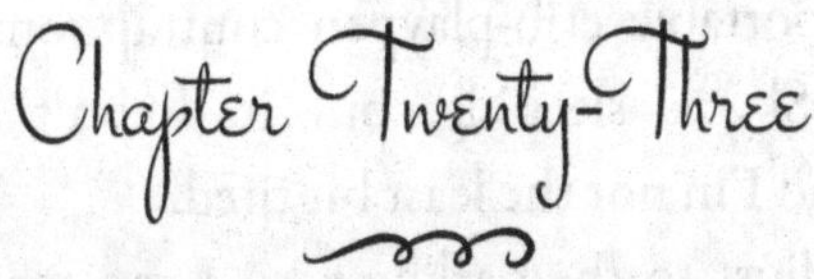

LEO

I let out the breath I've been holding once she pulls the blanket up over her shoulders and closes her eyes. I smile when I can hear her breathing, even and deep, not five minutes later.

Standing up with James in my arms, I walk over to the love seat, doing my best not to trip over all the crap on the floor. He certainly gave her a run for her money.

Holding a baby is something I've missed, but cleaning poop out of all those nooks and crannies? Not so much.

"Hey, little James, you're a stinker." He's smiling up at me as I smile back down and whisper to him, "You're a cute little stinker, though, aren't you?"

Yeah, diaper changes are all right. Just knowing you're making a little guy like him dry and comfortable again makes the smell something you can tolerate with a smile.

"Did you give your Aunt Skylar a hard time?" He gurgles and reaches for his feet. "Looks like you did."

I settle back into the recliner and let him finish off the rest of the bottle before I rest him on my chest and turn off the lamp.

"You must be just as tired as Sky is." He lets out a little burp, and when I check I see that his eyes are closed. There's one of those portable crib-playpen contraptions next to the couch where Sky is sleeping, but it doesn't look all that comfortable and I'm not the least bit tired.

My eyes adjust to the darkness, so I can make out Skylar sleeping peacefully just a few feet away from where I'm sitting.

Does she have any idea how beautiful she is? I've never seen her looking so worn out and disheveled, and even in this state, she's still the most desirable woman I've ever known.

When I saw James reaching his little hand up to touch her face and then the determined way he tried to get at her breast to feed, I felt a longing stir inside of me. Something primal, the most basic carnal need.

Poor thing was so tired she didn't know what she looked like. She didn't notice the wet spot his mouth left on her pink cotton tank top, the fabric so thin that I could see the outline of her nipple, pebbled and tight.

I want.

I want.

I want.

That's what plays on repeat in my head when I'm around her. I want to suck her right there on that wet spot, lick her sweet tits and cup them in my hands. I want to wrap her long hair around my fist, lean her back so that I can run my tongue along the column of her neck. I want her to touch me, to press her hand between my legs and ease this ever-present ache in my cock. And I want to push inside of her, to take what I need and make her mine.

Is it so crazy? She'll be twenty-two in a few months. She

had to submit identification to get on the list of people who can pick Libs up from school, and yeah, I looked. So she's not a kid, even though I've made a habit of calling her just that. And I'm twenty-nine. Seven years. Ok, almost eight years older. But is that so bad?

Damn, she just fits. I've been fighting my attraction to her since day one, been looking for faults that I just can't find.

And then there's Olivia. My daughter is crazy about her and I know the feeling is mutual. I hear the way Skylar speaks to my girl when she doesn't know anyone is listening. She's always looking to build her up, to shape her into the kind of person who loves herself, has confidence, and can handle whatever this life throws at you.

She's a better mother to Olivia than Olivia's mother ever was.

But therein lies the problem. Being with me means that Skylar will be taking on the role of Olivia's mother. Can't go back in time and date her like I would some other woman. She already has a strong bond with my daughter. She's already a part of our family.

Being in a relationship with a single parent is different. I'm a package deal. Choice doesn't factor into this. Any woman who's in my life is in Olivia's.

I'll be taking away the future Skylar has mapped out for herself.

Someone took from me once. Doesn't matter that it turned out well, that it turned out to be the best thing that ever happened to me. I won't do that to Skylar. I won't take from her because I know that she'll give.

It's just who she is.

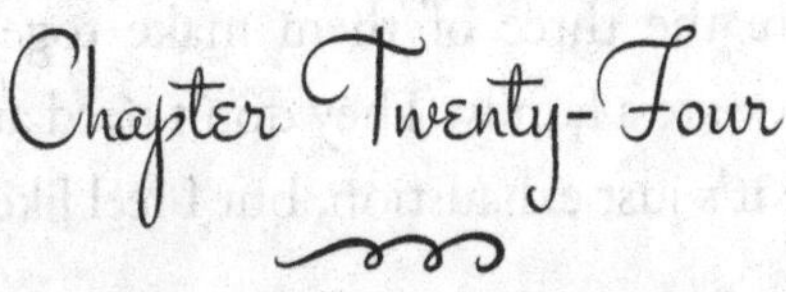

Chapter Twenty-Four

SKYLAR

"Do I look all right?"

"If you're asking me if you look like you hardly got any sleep this weekend, the answer is no. You look fine. What are you worried about?"

I shoot Leo a look. "I don't want them to think I couldn't handle it."

I flick a dishtowel his way when he has the nerve to smirk, and the doorbell rings at the same time.

I sound like a squeaky mouse when I say, "They're here!"

And the gig is up as soon as Garth and Sienna walk in the door and Olivia says, "James cry all the time."

"Libs, he didn't cry all the time." Looking to my sister, I confess, "He wouldn't take the bottle from me, Sienna. It got a little hairy."

"Oh," she rushes over to James and picks him up out of his seat. "Did you miss mommy? I missed you too!"

Garth shakes his head. "Next time he comes with us.

169

Sienna talked about him nonstop, and she was crying last night because he was," he uses air quotes, "so far away." He moves to stand behind Sienna and kisses James's head. "I missed you too, little guy."

The picture the three of them make together leaves me welling up. They are a family. They don't need anyone but each other. I'm sure it's just exhaustion, but I feel like an outsider in that moment.

I think Olivia senses my melancholy, and surprises me when she comes up and hugs me around my hips and tells me she loves me.

I love you.

She breaks my heart and builds me up whenever she says it.

I turn just in time to see the troubled look on Leo's face before he ducks out with some lame excuse about making a call for work.

It's Sunday.

He's not working.

He doesn't like the close attachment Olivia has formed with me, that's what I think. I get the feeling that it worries him. Or maybe it brings up a slew of painful memories related to his late wife.

Yeah, I'm thinking now is not the time to tell him what Olivia's teacher said after school on Friday.

He's missing in action for the next twenty minutes as we pack James up, Sienna and Garth tell me about their time up in Presque Isle, and Olivia gets a few extra minutes to love on the baby before they head out.

He gave them a quick goodbye before he left. He wasn't rude or anything, but it's awkward now. Something is different, something's off. But I use his absence as an opportunity to make sure I've set Olivia straight.

"Libs, come sit for a minute." She snuggles in next to me on the couch. "Remember what we talked about the other day after school, right?"

She won't answer. She's too busy scowling.

"I miss my mom, too. I understand what it's like."

"I want a mommy like Sarah and Clementine and Anna have mommies."

I feel like telling her you do *not* want a mom like Sarah's, but that's beside the point. "It's hard, I get that. But you are soooo lucky, Libs. You have the *best* dad. He loves you so much."

She wraps her arms around my waist. "And I have you."

I squeeze her right back. "You do have me. And if anyone asks, you can tell them I'm your special person. Just like you're super special to me."

She takes a deep breath, my stoic little sweetie. "But I can't tell people you're my mommy."

"You have a mommy, Olivia. Just because she's not here with you doesn't mean she's not your mom. Just like my mom. She's not here with me anymore but she'll always be my mother." She doesn't say anything but I can feel her head nodding against my middle. "So I'll see you tomorrow after school, ok?"

"You have to go?"

I roll my eyes and frown, heavy on the drama. "I have to do my homework and I have *two* tests this week. I need to study." Standing up, I reach for her hand. "Let's go to Dad's workshop so we can tell him I'm heading out."

I open the door to the garage. "Leo?"

He's leaning against his latest project, some classic Volkswagen van he's retrofitting with an electric motor. He doesn't have a tool in his hand. He's not even looking at the plans that are laid out on the work table. No, he's just staring at the wall, lost in thought.

"Leo? Um, I'm getting ready to go."

"Oh, hey. Right. Yeah, all right. Thanks for everything."

"Thank *you*. You were so great with James. You saved me last night."

Normally Leo would say something reassuring or he'd brush the compliment off. But he says nothing. He's not even listening to me right now.

"Ok. I'll see you tomorrow night."

"Uh, you know what...I'll get Olivia tomorrow after school. You've got finals this week, don't you?"

"Yes, but I've got it under control."

"You can take the entire week off if you want."

"No...I mean, I don't need time off."

"Let's just make plans for Tuesday then, ok?"

I feel like something is happening, but it's happening so fast that I can't make sense of it. "Yeah, I'll see you Tuesday at around ten-thirty."

His face is tight when he nods his head. "Good."

Maureen comes to relieve me Tuesday at dinnertime, not Leo.

"He said he has a thing with his friend Ed on campus." She lifts the lid off the pan on the stovetop. "Well, didn't I luck out tonight, Olivia? What did you two whip up today?"

"Chicken," Olivia answers with no enthusiasm.

"Libs," I force a cheery tone, "you've got to sell it. Chicken *marsala* with mushrooms and green onions over some *yummy* buttery noodles with parsley."

"And there's brussel sprouts," she adds with a pout.

"I happen to love brussel sprouts. And this smells fantastic." Looking to me, Maureen says, "Aren't you staying for dinner?"

I've already got my coat on. "Not hungry and I've got a final tomorrow. Gotta hit the books."

I'm not hungry but it's only because my stomach is in knots. Did the teacher talk to Leo yesterday? Is he mad about the whole Libs calling me mom thing? I would have told him but when I was leaving on Sunday he was acting weird, and I figured I had it under control anyway. Olivia seemed like she understood.

I lean in to give Olivia a kiss goodbye. "Wish me luck on my test, Libs. I'm off to the library."

"Good luck."

Her mood is off too. It's like there's a gray cloud hanging over this house. I look over to see this hasn't affected Maureen, though. She whistling a tune as she helps herself to a portion so big that I'm thinking there won't be much left over for Leo when he gets in.

Feeling kind of ornery as I walk out the door, I whisper so no one else can hear, "Serves him right."

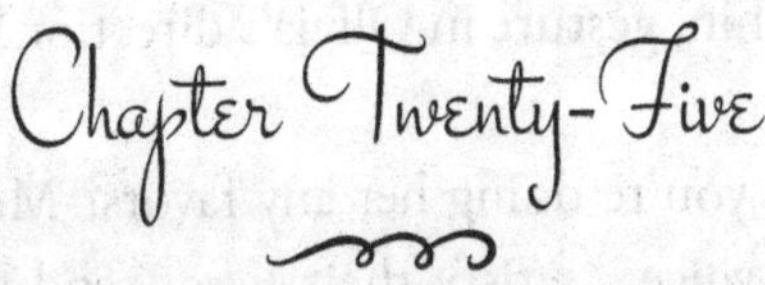

Chapter Twenty-Five

LEO

"You can cover Friday night? Sure it's no problem?"

"I've got nothing on my busy social calendar this Friday. But Saturday is a no can do. I have a date."

"Good for you."

She rolls her eyes. "Don't patronize me like I'm some old lady and the idea of me dating is amusing to you in some way."

"I wasn't."

"Yes, Leo, you were." Tossing the container of ice cream into the trash, the one that was full when I left this morning, she adds, "You could learn a few things from the gentlemen I date."

Here we go.

"You need to get out there. It's not natural, a young, good looking man like yourself without a partner. I'm not telling you to run out and find yourself a wife. I'm just saying...Put yourself out there for heaven's sake!" Turning to check herself out in the mirror she says, "Take it from me, if you don't use it you lose it."

Great, now I've got a visual of Maureen and some elderly dude doing the deed.

I raise my chin, gesture in Olivia's direction. "I've got other priorities."

"You think you're doing her any favors? Men who don't," she lowers her voice, "satisfy their *needs* tend to be miserable and grumpy. I'd say you fit that description."

I'm biting my tongue to keep myself from telling her to shut her trap. And while she fully deserves it, Momma didn't raise me that way. "Thanks for your concern, really, but I'm doing just fine." I don't know why I feel the need to add, "You'll be happy to know that I need you to babysit Friday night because I actually do have a date."

Her eyes light up. "I *knew* it! You're finally taking Skylar out?"

"What?"

"You know, Skylar, the very attractive young woman who spends a whole lotta time in your home. Ring a bell?"

"She, she..."

"She *what*?"

"Skylar works for me. That's all. I don't think of her that way. And what's the matter with you, Maureen?"

"Nothing's the matter with *me*," she says before picking a wayward cookie crumb off her shirt and popping it into her mouth. "Just pointing out what you're too blind to see."

"You're way off base." I check my watch then, hoping she'll get the hint that I want her gone.

She chuckles. "Don't get your undies in a twist. All right, I'm outta here. See you soon, kiddo."

Olivia barely turns her head away from the television when she mutters back, "Bye."

"Come on, Libs. Time for your bath."

She trudges up the stairs in silence and continues to sulk even though I dump nearly a full container of Mr. Bubble into the bath water.

"Is tomorrow school?"

"Yep. Wednesday is a school day."

"I don't wanna go to school."

"Why not? You love school."

"I hate it!" She slaps both hands into the water, sending little bubbles flying everywhere. "I hate school! I hate it!"

And then the tears come, angry and fast.

"Shh, shh. Hey, tell me what's going on. You always tell me you have so much fun in school."

Her face is red and splotchy when she cries out, "I don't have a mom!"

And I fall back onto my ass from where I'm crouched down because I don't think I've ever seen her this upset. Her cries turn into hiccups as I drain the water and rinse her off, all the while telling her it's all right, trying and failing to make her feel better.

She's quiet as I get her into her pajamas and so am I.

Mother's Day is a week from this Sunday. It's never come up before. On Mother's Day we usually video chat with my mom and call it a day.

We don't do any kind of memorial for Carrie, and now I'm thinking maybe that's been a mistake. I've never even gone to her see her gravesite since they put in the headstone. She's buried in Cincinnati, and there's nothing in that city for me except a mother-in-law I hope to never lay eyes on again.

Tucking her in and pushing her damp hair back behind her

ears I ask, "Are the kids making cards and stuff for Mother's Day?"

"Sarah says I don't have a mudder."

"Sarah's a jerk...I mean, that wasn't very nice of her to say. You do have a mother, she just happens to be in heaven. That boy in your class, Evan? His dad is in heaven too. I wonder if he gets sad around Father's Day."

She nods her head and sniffles. "And Nolan only has a grandma and a grandpa." Olivia fists the blankets in her little hands. "I made a card and I planted the flower seeds in the pot, but Sarah said I can't give it to Sky cause she's not my mom."

"You can give it to Sky if you want to. She's not your mom but—"

"She's my special person. That's what Sky says."

My lopsided smile matches my daughter's. "She is."

My special person.

And I'm right back to square one.

I made a decision. I shut down all those foolish thoughts I was having about a future with Skylar. Standing in the kitchen with her hair in a ponytail, looking like a sad and confused kid on Sunday, I had to get up and leave when Olivia went to her, comforted her and told Skylar she loved her.

It hit me with the force of a freight train.

Swooping in and planting myself into her life? I keep telling myself she's a woman—I've got the law on my side after all—but I'm lying to myself. She's still grieving a devastating loss, still figuring it out, still trying to find her place in this world.

I shake the guilt and the misery off before it can take hold. Tell myself that I need to lighten up.

I've already committed to having Skylar care for Olivia over the summer in between the two trips we'll take to Florida to see my parents, so there's that. But next year Sky will be student teaching while Olivia will be in full-time kindergarten. If she can just give me a few afternoons a week, that will be great. Make it easier. No sudden break, nothing that will hurt. The transition will be gradual.

Olivia will be all right, I'll make sure of it, and I can all but guarantee that Skylar will be better off for it in the long run.

My feelings don't factor into this equation. I just have to deal with it, I tell myself. Have to keep that part of my life compartmentalized.

That's the pep talk that led me to say yes when Max pushed this double date on me.

I shot him down straight away, but then relented when he called again on Sunday night assuring me she wasn't some club bunny just looking for a good time. Turns out Max is dating a nurse and her best friend is a lawyer. *You'll like Lexi*, he said. *She's nice, she's smart and she's hot.*

And she's not Skylar. That's what I was thinking, still freaking out from the aftermath of the weekend.

I flew back home early from Miami for one reason and one reason only: I wanted to see her.

I wanted to see Skylar and to be with her playing house in the home I built. And I wasn't disappointed. The mess and the cranky little fella aside, I felt something powerful when I walked in to see her holding a baby in her arms.

I wanted her to be mine, wanted her to be holding the child *we* made together. I wanted to walk in and do the whole *Honey, I'm home* routine.

Fucking ridiculous, that's how I felt Sunday morning in the cold harsh light of day.

I'll never see Olivia as anything but a light in my life, the absolute best thing that's ever happened to me, but in the eyes of your average twenty-something who's just starting out, I'm sure my life looks like a trap.

I'm bound by school schedules and bedtime routines. I don't take spur of the moment trips. I don't bar hop on the weekends, grab concert tickets last minute or try out the trendy new restaurants on the strip.

Skylar fits in my life. She'd make my life complete. But I don't fit in hers. It's a hard pill to swallow but it's the truth.

So even though I'm looking forward to Friday night about as much as I'd look forward to having a tooth pulled, I'll go. And I'll go into it with an open mind. I'll do my best not to think of Skylar as I'm sitting across from Lexi the lawyer.

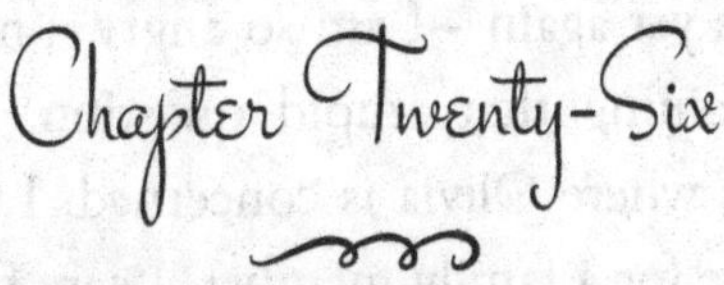

SKYLAR

And the cold war rages on.

Maybe I'm being paranoid. That's what I thought on Tuesday night when Maureen showed up to relieve me. But he texted to cancel on Thursday— no phone call—then left a voice message to tell me he was taking the day off on Friday. And the kicker? He sent a follow-up text to assure me that he'd *pay for my time.* Way to make me feel pathetic.

Absolutely not. I won't accept it. And it's fine. I need to get some studying done anyway.

He wrote: *When is your last final?*

And I felt like writing back: *Oh, we're making small-talk now?* But instead I just typed out: *Tuesday morning.*

He makes me feel like I'm a disease-carrying organism. Forget being in close proximity, I get the impression that even the sight of me is something he'd like to avoid at all costs.

It's a good thing I'm a decent student to begin with and that I haven't been slacking off this semester, because my ability to focus is shot to hell. I've sat in the library every day this week wondering what it is that I've done wrong.

Driving over to their house in my Sentra on Friday night—I discreetly dropped his car off with the keys yesterday when he cancelled on me yet again—I am so angry. I'm mad at myself for even entertaining that stupid question. I haven't done *anything* wrong where Olivia is concerned. I care for her the way I would care for a family member. I care for her the way I would care for my own child.

Maureen called me twenty minutes ago. She's babysitting tonight. *Oh, really?* I'm having an imaginary conversation with Leo as I drive. *So you tell me you're taking the day off and then ask Maureen to take care of Olivia? Maureen, the* hellion *you blame for all of Olivia's bad habits? What a liar, what a fraud you are.*

And when I walk in Maureen doesn't look the least bit under the weather. It's nearly eleven o'clock, and I'd much rather be in bed than be in this house right now.

"How are you feeling?"

"I'll make it, don't worry. I think Olivia and I just overdid it on the gummy worms. She's asleep upstairs and lover boy told me he'd be home by midnight."

"Lover boy?"

She rubs her palms together and smiles. "Hot date. Some young attorney from the area. And it's about time if you ask me. Young hunk of a man, all muscle and brawn. He's been living like a monk since that witch died."

"Maureen!"

"You didn't know her, I did. And how he wound up with her I'll never know."

"It just doesn't seem right to talk about Olivia's mother like that."

She waves me off. "Like I said, you didn't know her."

She's smiling again as she pushes her arms into her cardigan. "Our boy was dressed for success tonight. Sharp black button-down, black pants that he fills out quite nicely, *if* you know what I mean." Her expression is scheming in a creepy way, like this is some matchmaking gig we're both in on. Like I should be rooting for this bullshit along with her.

She practically skips to the front door. *Under the weather my ass.* "Thanks a bunch, Skylar."

I fall back onto the couch. "G'night, Maureen."

Of course he'd go for a lawyer. She probably specializes in patents or intellectual property law. She's no doubt smarter than me. More his equal.

He thinks of me as a kid. He's even called me *kiddo* before, same thing he calls Olivia. The last time he did it I was so tempted to remind him of the night we met—or didn't meet. I could have said something like: *You didn't call me kiddo when you had your dick pressed up against my ass. When you asked me if I liked it. Nope, I wasn't kiddo that night in the club.*

Now I'm hot and flustered thinking back to that night. I lay back on the couch and imagine him above me, caging me in and kissing me. But when I close my eyes thoughts of Leo with some other woman ruin it for me. I'm still hot all right, but it's jealousy stoking this fire, not lust.

I hear the key in the lock and note that it takes him a few tries before he's successful in opening the door. And is that a giggle I just heard? Did Leo Hale just...giggle? Swear to God, if he brought this chick home I'm going to pitch a fit. Last thing Olivia needs is to wake up to some strange woman in the house.

I stand up to face off with them but Leo is alone in the

kitchen. And the jerk has the nerve to stand there with a surprised look and a smile on his face when he sees it's me.

"Hi. This is a nice surprise."

He puts his keys down and walks over to get a glass of water from the sink.

"Aren't you going to ask what happened to Maureen?"

"What happened to Maureen?"

I'd like to slap him right now. "She called me to come over because she didn't feel well."

"Oh."

"That's it? Oh?"

"What...You think I should go check on her?"

"No. She seemed fine when I got here."

"Sorry she bothered you then."

I should go. He doesn't seem drunk but he's definitely had a few. *I should go*, I tell myself again, but I'm too damn mad. "Did you drive?"

"No, Mom. Took a car service."

"So I guess your hot date was a bust?"

He doesn't answer. Instead he walks over to the cabinet and takes a bottle down from the highest shelf. While I stand there waiting like a fool, he pours himself a small tumbler of some amber-colored liquid. He takes a seat at the kitchen table close to where I'm standing and sips his drink as he studies me.

A minute passes before he asks, "Hot date?"

"According to Maureen."

He nods his head, takes another sip. I can feel my face turning red from shame now rather than anger. I sound like a petulant baby, a shrew, and still I can't help myself.

"So where is she?"

"Had the driver drop her off first."

"Did you kiss her?"

"Might have pecked her on the cheek. Don't remember."

My tone is bitter, mocking. "Pecked her on the cheek?"

"Yeah." He looks annoyed now. "What should I have done?"

I shrug like I couldn't care less. "I'm just surprised, that's all. Knowing you, I figured you would have gone for it, given her a good night fuck."

His features harden as he stands and takes one step closer. "That's what you'd figure? Knowing me, huh? And what exactly do you know about me, sweetheart?"

I back up a step on instinct, but then cross my arms, ready to square off with him. I'm too angry and hurt to be intimidated. "Now I'm sweetheart? I'm not kiddo anymore? Sweetheart, is that what you called your lawyer tonight?"

"She's not my lawyer."

He takes another step closer and now I've got nowhere to go. My back is up against the kitchen counter and he's essentially got me caged in. I raise my chin in defiance but when I speak all that false bravado I had a moment ago is stripped away. "What is she to you?"

I hate the sound of my own voice. I sound hurt. I sound like a child.

"She's nothing to me."

I look down at the space between us, watch as his right hand moves slowly and lands on my hip. His thumb moves up and down, brushing just close enough to make me shudder. I want to look at him, to get a better handle on what's happening here, but I don't want to ruin this moment. If he's on the verge of losing control I'm not going to stop him.

I want some of whatever is in that crystal tumbler. I want to loosen up and be that girl I was in the club again. I want to turn my body around so that his front is pressed up to my back. I want to reach up and lace my arms around his neck and lean back into him, just like I did that night. I want him to remember. I want him to touch me the way he did that night, and this time I won't run away.

He leans down and angles his face like he's going to kiss me, but his mouth goes to my neck instead. His lips brush over the sensitive skin beneath my ear and then he breathes in deep. Every nerve ending in my body is on high alert, primed and ready for what comes next.

I take his hand and slowly guide it up from my hip, up the curve of my waist and to my breast. I lead him, cup it with him hand over hand, and when we make contact he lets out a quiet moan of desperation. He still doesn't kiss my lips but lays open mouth kisses down my neck, one by one to my collarbone. I'm practically shaking. I want his mouth on my tits and his hand between my legs so badly that I'm on the verge of begging.

Sliding my hand between us, I reach down to stroke him. Hard and eager, he moves his hips to urge me on. Up and down. Once then twice then—

"No." He backs up shaking his head. "I'm sorry. I shouldn't have done that."

My voice sounds small when I ask, "Why?"

"I just...I didn't mean to—"

"Touch me?" It's taking everything I have in me to keep from crying.

He backs up another step and turns away. "I'm so fucking sorry, Skylar. That was so wrong."

"Why is being with me so wrong? What's wrong with *me*?"

His eyes are soft when he turns back to face me. Two, maybe three feet separate us now, but we might as well be standing on two opposite shores with an ocean between us. He reaches across, puts a hand on my cheek, but I can't. I can't stand here and let him stutter through the speech he's about to make.

He's about to let me down easy, to tell me how wonderful I am and remind me of the bright future that's just waiting for me beyond the fucking horizon. That I'll have my pick of men to choose from someday. For good measure he might even throw in some nonsense about not being good enough for me.

He goes to open his mouth but I won't listen to this bull-shit. "Don't." I brush his hand off my cheek. "Don't say a word, and wipe that look off your face right now. I don't need your pity."

"Skylar."

It's almost comical, the way he says my name. He doesn't know what to make of this Skylar, doesn't know how to *handle* her. She's angry, and no one wants that, do they? He likes the Skylar who makes his life easy, who acts like she doesn't have a care in the world, who floats in and out with a smile on her face every damn day.

He acts like he's looking out for me, doing me a favor, that he knows better. I let out a cheerless laugh as I imagine what's going through his head right now. Maybe he thinks I'll look back on this moment ten years from now and say to myself, *You know what? Leo was right. Whew, I really dodged a bullet there.*

Every look, every time he says my name it stings, so now I want to hurt him back.

"You don't remember me from that night in the club, do you?"

I can see the wheels turning. A long minute passes before—jackpot!—the color begins to drain from his face. I've hit my mark and it feels good. So good that I can't stop.

"I know what your hands feel like, Leo. What you just did a

few minutes ago? You did a whole lot more out on the dance floor that night, didn't you?" I watch as he swallows, watch as he stands there struggling for something to say. My tone is hard when I command, "Look at me," and he obeys.

"You know every curve of my body. And I bet you still think back to that night. When you're all alone in that big bed I bet you touch yourself remembering exactly what it felt like. The weight of my breasts in your hands, my fingers fisting your hair." I fix my eyes on his on his crotch and see that he's still hard. "Do you still think about how good it felt to grind against me?"

He's shaking his head, so confused. He doesn't know who I am anymore and neither do I. This Skylar is hateful, she's bitter, and after the volcano inside of her is done erupting, she's just done.

I walk back to the living room and grab my bag from the couch. He calls after me when my hand is on the doorknob, "We need to talk."

I won't look at him, not now. "No, we really don't. I've been through much worse, Leo, so don't worry, I'll get over this. And don't you dare make any stupid decisions that will hurt Olivia. I'm still working for you. My feelings won't get in the way so don't sweat it."

My hands shake violently as I turn the key in the ignition and shift into gear. I drive slowly, so wound up that I know I have no business being behind the wheel right now. By the time I reach campus my breathing has evened out more or less, and I'm thinking more clearly.

He's probably going to fire me, and Lord knows he'd be justified. I raise up a silent prayer to God, as if He can control Leo and make him see reason. Still sitting there in the parking lot, I can't help but cry when I think about the potential fallout from what I've just done. I'm not tooting my own horn or anything when I think about Olivia, but I know she'll be devastated if I just up and vanish from her life. He won't do that to her. He can't.

My bag feels like it weighs a hundred pounds as I trudge up the stairs and open the door to my dark, quiet room. My roommate left for home yesterday after she took her last final. It was the flattest, most blah goodbye I've ever participated in. All this year, the two of us have just come and gone, saying hello and goodbye, polite and impassive. I feel the way I did in September. I feel alone.

I'll be going home after I watch Olivia on Tuesday *if* I still have a job. Right. And where is home? Is that what I call Garth and Sienna's place now? I'll stuff my bag into the back of James's closet, I'll sleep on the couch, I'll be taking up too much space and overstaying my welcome. They would never make me feel that way, I know that, but the truth is that I don't belong there.

It's only for two weeks. Figured I'd spend some quality time with James while Leo takes Olivia down to visit with her grandparents. Then I'm moving into an off-campus summer sublet with a friend of Simone's. A friend of a friend of Simone's would be a more accurate description.

The thought of that place does nothing to lift my spirits.

I was happy to find the last-minute house share until I pulled up outside to leave my deposit with the girl who arranged it. It looked like a frat house, with garbage littering the front yard and beat-up upholstered furniture on the porch that no one saw fit to protect from the elements. It smells like mold when you stand on the porch and weed once you step inside.

Holly—I only know her name from Simone's text—

followed the path my eyes took after she let me in. I'm guessing she was probably worried I was about to back out when she said, "We had a party last night. It doesn't normally look like this."

I took her word for it and handed over my share of the rent. *It's just a place to sleep*, I told myself. *I'll hardly be here at all.*

But now, flopping down onto my bed, I'm not sure what my immediate future looks like. Even if Leo does keep me on, is he going to pull what he did last week? Cutting my hours and making excuses because the mere sight of me makes him uncomfortable? I lay one arm over my face, trying to block out the image of that scene in the kitchen. If he was uncomfortable last Sunday after that non-event, imagine what he feels like now?

I try my best to shake it off and start with the positive self-talk. I tell myself Leo's a reasonable person, and above all else, that he loves his daughter. The odds of me being fired are low. And if he cuts my hours I'll find a second job. Keep busy, keep plugging along. That's what I'll do.

I don't have any other choice.

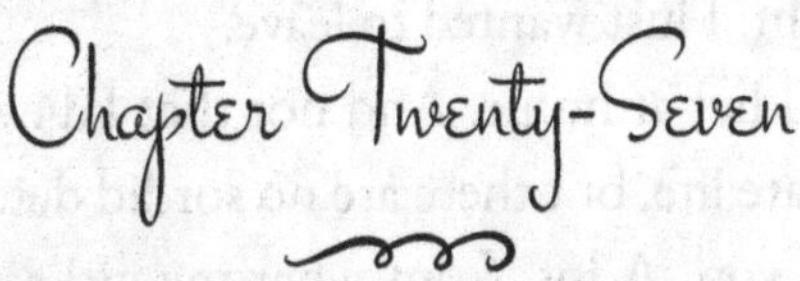

Chapter Twenty-Seven

LEO

I pull her text message up again, read it for what's probably the tenth time.

I was out of line last night. I'm sorry.

I don't know how to reply. I can't just write that it's fine, or *Let's just forget about it.*

Believe me, I'd give my right arm to develop a sudden case of amnesia right now, but I can't forget one word or one look that passed between us last night.

I hope she's not looking at her phone, because I've started typing and then stopped myself three different times. She'll be thinking the worst looking at the dialogue bubble popping up and then disappearing again and again and again.

I know I should call her, and I'm just about to bite the bullet when my phone starts ringing. Coward that I am, I'm actually relieved to see that it's Max calling.

"So how did it go after you two left last night?"

Max sounds hopeful, so I'm thinking I must have given off the impression that I was somewhat interested in Lexi. I don't see how that can be, though. My head was all over the place, to the point where I can't recall a single thing we talked about at dinner last night. I just wanted to leave.

"I dropped her at home. And not that I'd ever tell you shit about my private life, but there are no sordid details to report."

"She liked you. A lot, from what my girl says. I have four tickets to the Pirates game next Sunday so let's go...The four of us."

"That's Mother's Day. I'm taking Olivia out of school a few days before the term ends and flying down to Florida for two weeks. And," I pause for a second, "I don't think it's going to work out with Lexi. She was nice and I had a decent time, but I'm not looking for anything like that now."

"Like what? Sex, companionship, fun? Leo, you've been living like a monk for the past three years." *Four years*, I silently correct him. I stopped sleeping with Carrie once she told me she was pregnant. Her decision, not mine. "Just saying...Your junk is going to shrivel up and fall off if you keep going on like this."

"Nice visual. Thanks."

"Wait...Did you hook up last week when you were away in Miami? I knew it! You've been holding out on me, ya dog."

"Didn't hook up with anyone."

As long as you don't count the babysitter.

"You didn't shag that company rep you were telling me about?"

"Who?"

"The one from Jaguar who's been trying to lure you over to their team."

The one who's been emailing and texting non-stop? The one

who practically offered herself up on a silver platter for me last weekend?

"Sorry to disappoint, but no."

"Whatever, I'm just looking out for you. Hey, don't close the door on Lexi, on Miss Jag, or on anyone else right now. Just leave yourself open to the possibility of something good."

"If I didn't know any better I'd say you're in love, Max."

"You know what? I just might be."

"Yeah?" I'm legitimately surprised.

"Nadia is different. She's as fun-loving and easy as the women I usually go for, but I'm loving the fact that she's got her own thing going on. She's smart, has a good career, she's confident..."

"She seems great."

"She is. And I want that for you, Leo. I was joking before, but I mean it when I say that I'm worried you've been out of the game for so long. I get it, you have Olivia to worry about. And I'm not a parent, but I get that she's your top priority. But I think you shy away from meeting anyone new because of what Carrie did to you. Not every woman is Carrie."

It's taking everything in me not to unleash on him right now, so I end the call with some bullshit about keeping an open mind.

I didn't think it was possible to feel worse than I did before that call, but it is.

Not every woman is like Carrie. Translation: *Not every woman is a dishonest gold digger out to screw you over.*

That's how Max sees her. He was the only person who warned me off her in the very beginning. And when I was going through the worst of it, caring for an infant in the aftermath of Carrie's death, scared out of my damn mind that I might lose Olivia—that she might not be mine—I didn't have any kind thoughts to spare where my wife was concerned either. But that burning hatred I had for Carrie has started to fade. The years have lessened the sting of what she put me through.

I know that being angry at Max for speaking ill of Carrie makes me a hypocrite. I still say those words to myself sometimes, still look at the picture in my daughter's room and tell that woman that I hate her. But now I also tell myself that there are good and bad in all people. And she was twenty-five when she died. How sad is that? We may have ended under the worst possible circumstances, but Carrie wasn't evil and I don't like talking about her that way.

"Daddy, look at this."

Turning to see my little girl coming down the stairs, who's sure to be the spitting image of her mother someday, I can't feel anything but love. I'm not all the way there, but all that bitterness and hate is slowly giving way to gratitude.

"Whatcha got there?"

"It's for Skylar."

"You're getting to be a great artist, Libs."

Pointing to each figure she says, "That's me and that's Skylar."

I'm focused on the sun taking up a prominent amount of space on the front of the card and the tiny hearts she drew all around the figure that is obviously Sky.

"This is nice. I think she'll be really happy when you give it to her."

"I'm gonna give it to Sky on Mudder Day."

I smile to myself listening to that one last remnant of baby talk she's still struggling with. She sounds out the *th* fine in some words, but mother and father always trip her up. She sounds so cute that it takes me a second to process what she said.

"On Mother's Day?"

Should I remind her again that Sky isn't her mother? That this isn't appropriate? I just don't have it in me.

"Libs, we're going to be in Florida with Grammy and Grampy on Mother's Day. Remember? We get to ride on the big plane this Wednesday."

Her eyes light up. "I forgot!" Wiggling off my lap and heading back upstairs she says, "I gotta make Grammy a card, too!"

"Good idea. And you just reminded me I have to buy Grammy a card and shop for something special."

She stops in her tracks and then turns. "And I'll give Sky her card on Special Person Day."

"When is that?"

"Today!"

"Uh, no Libs. Sky doesn't come here today."

"Tomorrow?"

"No, and she has a test the day after tomorrow." Her smile drops and my heart sinks along with it because I know that seeing Skylar before we leave means...I'm going to have to see Skylar before we leave. Fuck me. "She's coming here on Tuesday and that's the day before we go to Florida. Is that good?"

"Yes!" And then she rattles off her crazy list of things to do as she takes the stairs one by one. "I make Sky a cake. A present. I make a Happy Grammy Day card..."

I've got a pit in my stomach the size of a boulder. I look to where my phone sits on the table. *You're eventually going to have to talk to her so just do it.* I reach for it and then put it back down again. *This isn't going to get any easier so stop being a pussy.*

I'm praying it goes to voicemail when she picks up. I can hear her take in a deep breath before she says hello, which tells me she's not exactly jazzed that it's me on the other end of the line.

Now I'm thinking I should have planned this out a little better because I don't have a clue right now. I don't know what to say and she obviously doesn't either. An uncomfortable moment passes before I say, "I got your text." I clear my throat because I'm really fucking nervous right now. "I'm the one who's sorry."

"I feel awful."

"You shouldn't," I tell her. "You didn't do anything wrong."

"I shouldn't have spoken to you that way."

"Sky...I just...I never knew it was you. I'm sure you know that...I mean, I hope you do. And I'm beyond ashamed of myself that I laid a hand on you last night...That I ever laid a hand on you." It suddenly occurs to me to ask, "This whole time, did you know it was me? That I was the guy you danced with that night?"

The guy you danced with. I go with that instead of *the guy who groped you like a perv.*

"No, not at first. One night when you were washing the dishes you pushed your sleeves up and I saw the tattoos on your left arm. That's when I knew."

"Oh."

"So where do we go from here?"

She's asking the million dollar question. "I don't really know. Do you still feel comfortable working here? If you don't, I'd totally understand."

Her voice trembles when she asks, "Do you *not* want me to work with Olivia anymore?"

"Sky, you know I think you're great with Olivia." I hesitate for a second before adding, "You're the best thing that's happened to our family in a long time. I hope you know that."

She takes in a shaky breath. I can picture what she looks like right now. I can see her twisting her hair like she does when she's uncertain, can see her sad eyes, and I'm so angry with myself because I've done this to her. I've hurt her.

"I'd like to keep my job if it's ok with you."

"Of course it is. And you and me...Can we go back to where we were? I swear I'll never cross that line again."

I feel sick having to say it again. To assure this girl that I won't put my hands on her.

"Yeah, Leo. We can go back to where we were."

"Maybe this trip to Florida is coming at a good time."

"Yeah."

I try my best to sound more upbeat, you know, more like everything is suddenly just fine and back to normal. "You're coming over on Tuesday after your test, right? I mean, if you want to just get on the road that's fine. I don't need childcare that day, really. It's just that Olivia's got some big surprise for you. She's taking the special person thing to another level." I keep rambling. "I think she's going to petition for it to be recognized as a national holiday or something."

"A surprise?"

"Yeah." I feel like I need to prepare her. "She made you a card and I think she wants to make you a cake...Like a quasi Mother's Day thing. Is that all right?"

A moment passes before she says, "Sure. Ok, so I'll see you Tuesday."

"Thanks."

I'm about to tell her that I'm sorry again, but stop myself. I still wish I could go back in time and undo what happened last night, but I'm pretty sure I'm going to scare her off if I keep groveling and apologizing.

And fuck me, I can't stop thinking about it. Can't stop replaying the things she said to me. *You know every curve of my body.*

I feel like a sick man when I think back to that night last year, touching her without even knowing her name. *Do you still think about how good it felt?* I picture myself with my hand on a bible, under oath, having no choice but to answer that I do. Yeah, I think about it all the time when I'm *all alone in that big bed.* Fuck, that stung.

And then I have to fully acknowledge that I *am* a bastard because the memory of our bodies pressed together along with the memory of her hand stroking me last night has me growing hard again.

I call out to Olivia that I'm taking a quick shower, all the while knowing that I'm going to let myself live in that moment again, telling myself: *Just one last time.*

As steam fills the room and the hot water pours down on me, I settle in and let my mind wander. I imagine Skylar's face and the way she looked when I moved in close, the low moan that escaped when I touched her, her eager lips looking for mine to kiss hers.

In the shower I don't push her hand away when she touches me. No, I cover her small hand with mine and show her how to make me feel good. I kiss her, let myself taste what I've wanted for so long. And when she gets down on her knees in front of me, I watch as she wraps her lips around me and takes me inside. Then I can't see anything, can't feel anything but the firm grip I have on myself as I pump my hips pretending that it's her mouth I'm moving in and out of.

It doesn't take long, and fuck it, this time I won't let myself feel bad about it. I give myself permission to lose myself in it, to acknowledge that it feels so much better than good because this is the last time. I won't let myself do it again.

Go back to where we were.

Yeah, the road to hell is paved with good intentions.

Chapter Twenty-Eight

SKYLAR

Go back to where we were. Where exactly is this fantasyland?

I'll never be able to go back to thinking of Leo as my employer, as Olivia's father and nothing more. And while I know I'll just have to suck it up and pretend, the foolish woman who lives inside of me doesn't want to.

I collapse back onto my bed after hanging up. I barely slept last night, and that call took every last remaining speck of energy out of me.

He was right about one thing. Their trip to Florida and my trip home couldn't be coming at a better time. Two weeks for this tension between us to ebb, two weeks to get my head back on straight, two weeks to forget about the possibility of anything happening where Leo is concerned.

I'm pretty much exhausted by the time I pull up outside of their house. It's only ten-thirty in the morning but I haven't had a good night's sleep in days—not since that disastrous, humiliating, oh so awkward exit I made on Friday night.

How exactly does one look their employer in the eye after groping his dick? That's the question I've been pondering for the past couple of days.

My tests are over with, papers handed in, so now I just have to get through the next hour or so before I can get on the road and let time start to heal this open, gaping wound.

"Surprise!"

I came in with my game face on, but just one look at Olivia with her big hopeful smile, and damn, I'm watering up again.

Jeez, I *never* used to cry.

I take in the room with the balloons, the flowers and the pink frosted cake, smiling as I wipe at those few stray tears.

"What's all this?" I ask her.

"It's my special person day!"

I take a seat at the kitchen table and open my arms for her to climb onto my lap. "This might be the nicest thing anyone's ever done for me." I hug her close. "Thank you, Libs. You're my special person, too."

I don't see him standing there until he clears his throat and says, "Olivia, did you bring the card downstairs?"

Her eyes go wide. "I be right back."

I want to squeeze tight and beg, *Please don't go, Olivia!* but she's already running up the stairs so I have no choice but to face him and face the music.

"Hey."

"Hi. This is, um, really nice. Thank you."

"Libs basically did everything. I just drove her around and followed orders." He shifts on his feet and swallows. "Listen, I just want to tell you again that I'm—"

"Don't say it again. You don't need to. Let's just do what we said we're going to do...Move past it."

He lowers his head and nods.

"You can go get some work done or pack or do whatever you need to do. I'll hang out with Olivia for a while before I get on the road."

"Are you sure?"

"Yeah."

He lets out a breath—relieved or sad, I can't tell which. "All right. I'll just be in the garage. Let me know whenever you want to get going."

But he lingers and watches as Olivia bounces back into the kitchen with her artwork.

She hands it to me and then clasps her little hands behind her back, waiting on my reaction.

It's a picture of the two of us with her hand in mine. She's taken care with it; this is more elaborate and detailed than the pictures she usually draws. My head is encircled in a halo of miniature hearts and she's glued multi-colored glitter around the edges to make a special border. We're both wearing smiles and there's a big sun, so bright and yellow that I can almost feel the warmth radiating from it.

I press it to my chest, careful not to bend or damage the paper in any way. "Olivia, I love it. I think this is my favorite of all the pictures you've ever drawn."

Her smile lights me up from the inside. "Really?"

"Yes, really. I'm going to get a frame for it and hang it in my bedroom."

From the corner of my eye I see Leo slip from the room.

"I frosted the cake myself. Daddy helped but I did it."

"It looks sooo delicious. Can I have a piece?"

"Yes." She walks over to the drawer and gets a butter knife, making a show of holding it the way I taught her, point down. "Let's cut you a piece." She's role-playing, turning the tables on me and acting like she's in charge. "Can you get two plates, Sky?"

I set the knife she's holding down on the table. "Yes, ma'am."

"Thank you. And Sky, do you want milk or water?"

"Ooh, with cake? A nice cold glass of milk."

"Coming right up!" And I smile listening to her spot-on imitation of me.

I get the glasses as she hefts the container of milk from the refrigerator and sets it on the table.

"This is so nice," I tell her as we cut the cake with my hand over hers.

"I know. It's a special day." Her expression is serious when she adds, "It's not mudder day."

I nod. "It's a day for the other special people in your life."

She nods but I can tell she's troubled. She lets it go, though, focusing on the giant mouthful of cake perched on her fork. And then she's smiling again, with pink frosting caught in the corners of her mouth.

"This is sooo good, Olivia. Did you know pink frosting was my favorite when you made this cake?"

"I know pink is your favorite color." I didn't know that but I nod and just go with it. "It was my mommy's favorite color, too."

"It was?"

She bobs her head up and down with a full mouth. After a few chews she says, "She liked pink dresses and," she points to her own hair, "pink clips."

"You look like your mom…A lot. She was really pretty just like you are."

"I know," she answers without missing a beat.

"So, you're going away tomorrow. That's so exciting, taking a ride on a plane."

"You ever been on a plane?"

"No." She looks at me with wide eyes. "Someday soon I will. Maybe I'll take another trip to New York. I've been there before but my mom and dad drove us all the way there."

"I want to go to New York."

"It's so much fun. When Sienna and I went with our parents we saw *Mary Poppins* in a big Broadway theater with red velvet seats. We ate in fancy restaurants and we rode in a carriage through Central Park, just like Cinderella. Oh, and we went to the racetrack and saw the horses run. They had the best hot dogs there. We ate ours piled with sauerkraut and mustard."

She scrunches her face up. "Mustard...Eww!"

I dab a bit of leftover pink frosting on her nose. "Different strokes for different folks."

As she wipes the frosting off her nose and licks it off her fingers, I'm overcome for a moment there, just taken by how sweet and loving a gesture this was. Looking around the kitchen again, I'm amazed that she did all of this for me.

The realization strengthens my resolve to make it work. I'll suck it up for Olivia's sake and for Leo's. He's been through enough.

I don't know what Maureen was going on about the other night, but I can't take what she said to heart. Doesn't matter if they had a perfect marriage or an imperfect one. At the end of the day, he lost his wife and the mother of his child. I need to remember that.

Chapter Twenty-Nine

LEO

I hang back, not wanting to interrupt the moment the two of them are having.

When I heard mention of Olivia's mother I stood down, kept to the garage but left the door open. Out of curiosity mostly. I don't seem to have a clue as to how to talk to my daughter about her mom, so maybe if I listen in I can learn something.

My heart feels like there's a weight on it listening in as Skylar tells Olivia about her own mother. About the way she'd set her hair in rollers and put make-up on before she went out on Friday nights with her father. She makes it sound special and glamorous, and to a kid that's how your parents seem when they dress up and hit the town.

Skylar goes on to tell her all about the trip to New York she took as a child. And I know that if I peeked my head in, I'd see my daughter sitting across from her idol transfixed.

I could never could put my finger on it, the reason I liked

listening to her talk myself, but now I realize it's because she seems to inject everything with life.

Sky doesn't just tell Olivia that she took a carriage ride on a chilly spring night. She makes the image come to life imitating the clop-clop sound the horses hooves made on the ground as they pranced through Central Park, the fancy top hat the driver with the big red nose wore, and the carriage blanket that reeked of wet hay and possibly manure. I almost laugh out loud at Olivia's reaction when she learns the meaning of that word.

Nearly twenty-two and she's never been on a plane. Olivia's still a few months shy of her fifth birthday and she's jetted back and forth to Florida more times than I can count.

For a hot minute I entertain the idea of taking them both to New York for Olivia's birthday in September. We'd cut the six-plus hour drive she took years ago to an hour and twenty on a plane. I could get tickets to a Broadway show, take them on a boat tour up the Hudson like my parents did with me, have high tea at The Plaza like the character in Olivia's Eloise books. Dirty water dogs from those sidewalk carts? Not a chance. I'd take her—I mean them—to upscale spots and places that would blow their minds.

I shake my head, knowing I'm playing a fool's game. Knowing I'm weak when it comes to Skylar. I just vowed that I was going to shut this ridiculous bullshit down, and here I am daydreaming about being the man who gets to show her things, teach her about all the world has to offer, treat her the way she deserves to be treated.

When I walk into the kitchen, ready to wrap this up out of my own selfish need for distance, I stop in my tracks when I hear Olivia ask Skylar about Mother's Day.

Skylar sees me and then turns back to Olivia. "I was just

telling Libs that this Mother's Day is special in my family because it's Sienna's first one now that she's a mom."

Olivia looks to me with a very serious expression. "And she gonna go see her own mom."

"I'm going to see the stone Garth made for her," Skylar clarifies. She stands and starts to clear the plates. I don't even realize she's talking to me when she asks, "Remember the diner I sent you to when we visited the baby?"

"Yeah," I recover, still confused.

"The hardware store where Garth works is right across the street."

"I remember seeing it."

"Garth's boss, Mr. Roberts, is a great guy. He worked as a mason before he opened the store and he's a stone engraver too. He's been teaching Garth how to do it. Apparently it's a decent side gig and Garth is always looking for ways to make extra money. So his first job," she bestows on me the first real smile I've seen in days, "that he's not making *one penny* on, was to make a headstone for my parents."

"She's gonna put flowers there."

"Yep. And I was telling Libs that my mother's favorite color was purple so I'm thinking of planting a few small hyacinths around the stone."

"Cause they smell good."

She looks to Olivia with wide eyes. "They actually smell *so* sweet you'd think they were candy."

"Really?" Olivia is mesmerized.

"They really do. I'll bring one for you to plant in the back-yard when you get home from Florida."

"Ok."

Now Olivia is back to sporting that same look. The troubled look she has whenever Carrie or the mention of mothers in general come up.

Skylar reaches down and pulls Olivia into a hug, whispering in her ear that she'll miss her but she'll see her soon.

"Remember what you have to do?" Skylar asks as she gathers her things getting ready to leave.

Olivia nods dutifully. "Tell Mickey and Minnie Skylar says hello."

Skylar nods the same way, as if this is truly serious business. "You might even run into Elsa. Wouldn't that be awesome?"

I'm about to tell Sky that I've already got it covered, that I went and booked some princess brunch package that sounds absolutely brutal. I want to pop an aspirin just thinking about the inevitable sea of screaming little girls packed into a dining hall with their families eating crappy buffet food. And I also shelled out for the most expensive hotel just because it's rumored that a character from *Frozen* makes an appearance at eight o'clock to read a bedtime story. But that's a surprise I have to keep to myself for now.

"You love Elsa, too." Olivia is full on pouting now. "I wish you could come."

When I start thinking about how much more fun we'd have if Skylar did come along, I shake my head in an effort to shut it down. I realize too late that Skylar sees the gesture and mistakes it for something else.

The hurt look is gone in a flash, though, replaced by the sunny smile she typically sports. "That's on my bucket list, Libs. I want to see a blue-footed booby in the Galapagos Islands," this gets a giggle from Olivia, "walk the cobblestone streets in Croatia and pretend I'm Arya Stark from *Game of Thrones*," that earns one from me, "ride a camel at sunset around the pyramids in Giza *and* take pictures with my favorite characters in Disney World."

After one more quick hug for Olivia and a quick, *Have a great trip*, aimed at me, she's off. I call after her, offer the Mercedes, but she just shakes her head and keeps on walking down the driveway.

Everything about this is wrong. I feel like everything I do is a misstep, and everything I say comes out sounding so awkward that it's misconstrued.

I'm getting everything wrong.

SKYLAR

Looking at him in disbelief, I ask, "What has it been, three weeks? I can't believe how big he's gotten!"

James is standing on my lap as I hold him steady, pushing off with his legs and bouncing. And he obviously finds this new superpower hilarious because he's smiling and giggling with every blast-off. My nephew is so freaking adorable.

Sienna laughs and covers her face. "I asked the doctor about it last week. Told him James was three months old and standing already, and then asked if it was normal." She's smiling shaking her head. "Yeah, he schooled me." Pointing to James, she says, "That doesn't constitute standing or even being able to bear weight on his legs at all. I felt like such a new mom."

Garth comes in and sits beside me, tickling James's belly. "He is a month ahead of schedule for doing this, though. I looked it up online. You gonna rule the gridiron like your daddy did in high school, little man?"

"Oh, lordy," I tease. "Are you about to go all *Glory Days* on me right now?" I start humming Bruce's tune.

"Don't listen to her," he says to James. "She was just a cheerleader."

"Ooh, burn. I am *so* not offended right now, but nice try." I look to Sienna. "Have you seen anyone from school recently?"

Garth reaches for James so I hand him over. "Are you asking if we've seen Tyler?"

"No. I was legit asking if you've seen any of our old friends. But since you brought him up, how's he doing?"

"I actually think he's turned a corner. His Uncle Paul—"

"The one who worked on the oil rig in Texas?"

He nods. "Still does, but he's back home for a bit...Think he was furloughed. Anyway, he's a recovering alcoholic and he's been steering Tyler in a better direction." He looks up to Sienna and something passes between them before he adds, "He's been going to Gambler's Anonymous meetings. Just got his one-month keychain."

"His what?"

"It's a twelve-step program just like AA. They give out sobriety chips to mark milestones, and I guess GA runs kind of similar."

"Wow." I pinch the bridge of my nose, fighting off this sudden urge I have to cry. I'm so sad for Tyler but happy for him at the same time. "That's good," I tell Garth.

"And he stopped drinking...Not that I ever thought he had a problem with it. Guess it's just easier to slip up when you've got a buzz on or you're in the bars watching Monday Night Football or whatever."

"What about—"

Sienna finishes my thought for me. "Lila?"

Garth smiles. "He finally wised up and dumped her ass."

Looking to Sienna wide-eyed, he corrects himself, "I meant to say he dumped her butt, didn't I, James?"

"He still asks about you, Sky. But it's different now...Just like he truly wants to know if you're all right." Sienna looks to gauge my reaction before adding, "He seems genuinely happy when I tell him you're doing well."

I let that sink in for a minute. "Maybe we're forever connected to the important people from our past. I mean, I don't ever see me and Tyler getting back together again, but I know I'll still think about him from time to time and he'll always have a place in my heart."

"I agree with you." Sienna perks up again because, you know, Sally Sunshine just can't help it. "Oh! Garth and Mr. Roberts installed the stone a few days ago. It came out so great!"

"It's *adequate*, baby, and that'll have to be good enough for now. Once I get better at it I'll make two stones to replace it."

"I'm sure you did a great job, Garth. And when Sienna told me about the design I kind of liked the idea of one stone for the two of them."

"I only did that because it was cheaper. I intend to replace it."

"Do you want to go see it now?"

I shake my head and smile at Sienna. "I'd rather wait until Sunday."

She understands.

"That's nice, Leo giving you two weeks off after finals."

"He's away with Olivia anyway so it just worked out. Are you guys sure I won't be in the way?"

"Not a chance!" The two of them say it at the exact same time and then laugh.

"Where did they go?" my sister asks.

"Florida. Leo's parents retired down there. I think they're older so they don't travel up north much anymore. He takes her down to see them a couple of times a year. The four of them are hitting Disney World for a few days this time."

Sienna's eyes light up. "I cannot wait to take James to Disney!"

"Just say the word, baby. I'll book us a trip whenever you want."

I'm about to tell Garth that's it's wildly expensive and that they can't afford it. Hell, they can't even afford the park tickets, let alone a hotel and the gas money they'll need to drive to Florida. But it's not my place and I know that, so I take a different angle instead. "James won't even know where he is now. I'd wait until he's five or six and he's gotten the chance to see a few of the movies."

"You're probably right," my sister says, and her eyes tell me she's grateful to me for not bursting Garth's bubble.

"And," I tell Garth smiling, "like it or not, I'm coming along, so you have to wait until I at least finish school next year."

He holds James's hand up for a high-five. "Sounds like a plan."

Chapter Thirty-One

LEO

I let out a breath once Skylar takes off for the night, even though the sight of her walking out my front door leaves me feeling more disappointed than relieved.

The entire time we were in Florida I was stressing out over what it would be like when I saw her again, but today went well. It wasn't awkward, the conversation wasn't strained, I got a ton of work done on a project I started with Ed, and I even got around to opening the pool.

When they came back from the park and saw me skimming the water, Olivia started jumping up and down like a lunatic. She spent more time in the pool down at my parents' condo than anywhere else.

I still don't trust her around the water, but I feel better knowing Skylar will be the one supervising her rather than Maureen. Nope, try as I might, I cannot picture Maureen sprinting out to the backyard and executing a swan dive to save someone in distress.

"Your friend...Grace? She said you used to be a lifeguard. Is that true or was she pulling my leg?"

"Grace wasn't teasing about that. I worked as a lifeguard for two summers." She turns to Olivia. "You know what that means, Libs? Swim lessons starting tomorrow."

"I know how to swim. Right, Daddy?"

"You were doing pretty good at Grammy and Grampy's, but remember what I said?"

She nods. "I gotta be expert before I can go in the water alone."

Skylar tosses in, "I'd also say you have to be at *least* eight years old before you can go in alone. Got it?" Olivia nods her head. "And this will be fun! I'll teach you how to swim freestyle like a crocodile, breast stroke like a sea turtle, and to swim on your back like an otter."

"I can do that!" she says with pride. "Daddy teached me how to float on my back."

"He *taught* you how to float? That's great!"

It's not lost on me the way Skylar takes every single moment and turns it into an opportunity to teach Olivia something. She never corrects her language, just models the proper way to say the word. Come to think of it, she never makes people feel like they're doing wrong, just shows them through her words and her actions how to do it better.

By the end of the week I realize she's been schooling me, too. Skylar's been the consummate professional. You'd never know anything went down between us just a few weeks ago. She's moved past it. Either that or she's a damn good actress.

Maybe Skylar is an expert at compartmentalizing her life. Maybe she's put me in a box marked *not happening* and moved on. If she has then kudos to her. Lord knows I've been trying to do just that and failing miserably.

She leaves right after the three of us eat dinner together on Friday night. I should be glad things are getting back to normal, that's what I keep telling myself, but the house feels so quiet and empty every time she walks out the door.

"Did you learn anything new today, Libby?"

"Hmm..." She does this cute thing now where she puts a finger on her chin whenever she's thinking. "I floated like the otters. Oh, and I paddled like a doggy to safety swim." She shows me how she raises her head high while paddling her hands in quick strokes.

I noticed before that Skylar used zip ties to fasten the floaty noodles I keep in the shed onto each stair railing, giving Olivia something to reach for in case she ever finds herself struggling in the water.

"Were you able to swim to the noodles?"

"Yep!"

"That's great."

"Daddy, I want a purple lavender bathing suit like Skylar."

"You don't like the suits Grammy bought you in Disney?"

She shrugs even though she was out of her mind happy with those suits just a week ago. "I like Skylar's better."

Skylar took Olivia shopping with her the morning after I opened the pool. She didn't bring any bathing suits from home, she said, and figured she needed a few new ones for the season.

The suit Olivia is referring to is a favorite of mine, too. It's about as simple as it gets, a one-piece with straps that criss-cross over her back. It's not too low cut in the front or high cut on the bottom. It's actually modest compared to what you see on the beaches these days, but she looks like a goddess in it.

Long legs, posture as straight as a ballerina's, the subtle curves of her hips and breasts. I had to look away when I first caught sight of her coming out of the pool, rendered stupid from one look at that body with her long hair dripping wet down her back.

Olivia tugs on the hem of my shirt as if to say: *Uh, hello, earth to Dad.*

"I can ask Skylar to help me look online for a kid-sized one that looks like it, ok?" When she nods, I go back to loading the dishwasher but there's a knock on the door.

"Max?"

"Hey! Haven't seen you since you got back and we were just in the neighborhood for happy hour at that new craft brewery on Shady. Figured we'd pop in."

We includes Max, Nadia and Lexi the lawyer. He called me a few days ago, and when I told him I was busy getting the pool opened he mentioned a barbecue referencing *the girls* like we're a foursome. I blew him off, so right now he's being an annoying prick, which is his idea of being helpful.

He walks past me. "Hi, Libby."

"Hi, Max," she answers, fist bumping my friend like they're best buds. "Who's that?"

"This," he pulls Nadia in close, "is my girlfriend, Nadia, and this beautiful lady is Lexi, a friend of your dad's."

Olivia looks to me. "You got a girlfriend?"

I shoot Max a look. "Lexi is a friend of mine." I walk over and give her a total bro hug, like with no bodily contact whatsoever, then introduce her to my baby. "Lexi, this is my daughter, Olivia."

"Oh my God, aren't you *so* cute!" Olivia smiles at Lexi while simultaneously managing to look confused. I want to tell Libs: *I feel you* because I don't know what the hell is going on either.

Lexi takes a seat at the table and starts peppering Olivia

with questions. And while I'm engaged in a half-hearted conversation with Max and Nadia, I hear my daughter reference Skylar in nearly every response she gives. Who gave you that beautiful bracelet? *Skylar.* Look at these adorable blond curls! You're so lucky! *I want brown hair likes Skylar's.* This goes on for a few more exchanges before Lexi abandons Olivia and walks over to us laughing. "Who is this Skylar she keeps talking about?"

I answer, "Her babysitter," at the same time Olivia pipes up and says, "She's my special person."

Lexi keeps smiling but her words come out sounding sarcastic when she says, "She must be *really* special."

Max pokes his head into the refrigerator. "So, are you going to offer us a drink?"

"Yeah, sure," I answer, even though I really want to tell the three of them to beat it. You can't drop by unannounced on parents with little kids. It screws up the whole nighttime routine. But Max doesn't know this and neither do the girls. "I have this IPA," I nudge him out of the way and show them one of the bottles, "or Bud."

I look up at the clock as I open the bottles, and seeing as it's only seven o'clock, I know Olivia won't shut it down for the night just yet. Skylar's been teaching her the basics of time and numbers, and while Libs doesn't have anything close to a clear understanding of it, she does know that an eight on the digital clock means bath, book and bedtime, while seven means: *Don't even think about trying to put me to bed.*

Two hours later Olivia is hopped up on the cookies Max keeps passing her way, even though I've told him to knock it off twice. She's putting on a show fueled by sugar now, dancing around the living room and singing along to the soundtrack of *Oklahoma.* Yep, Skylar's introduced her to the world of musical theater. Meanwhile, the three party crashers are happy and tipsy, egging Olivia on.

When she starts belting out *O-K-L-A-H-O-M-A* at the top of her lungs with the letters out of order for the third time in a row, I cut her off. "Olivia, that's it. It's past your bedtime. Say goodnight to everyone and let's go upstairs."

"*Nooo!*" Nadia and Lexi whine in unison. Lexi says, "C'mere, Olivia," and grabs my daughter into a hug while smiling up at me. "Let her stay up. She's *so* adorable."

I've been nursing this one beer all night, so I'm not finding Lexi's act one bit cute or amusing. "Nope. Libs will be a crank tomorrow if she doesn't get her sleep."

"I *won't* be a crank!"

Forget using her indoor voice to protest, that shrill squawk is a voice I'm well-acquainted with and one that fills me with dread. Yep, she's on the verge of a meltdown.

I hoist Olivia over my shoulder as she starts to cry and rain blows down on my back with her tiny fists.

"Aw," Lexi pouts as Max grabs another round of beers from the fridge and leads them out onto the back deck. "Goodnight, Libs," she calls after us, and the nickname sounds so wrong coming from her.

Don't call her that, I want to yell back. *You don't even know her.*

I'm just reaching the top of the stairs when there's a knock on the door. *What now?* I'm tempted to ignore it when the knocking starts up again, loud and persistent.

"What's up, Mr. Carey?"

Rob is the most irritating guy on my block. The only irritating guy, really. I like the rest of my neighbors, and we all kind of feel the same way about Rob. He's the one who not so subtly lets you know if your grass is getting too long or if your paint is starting to chip. His house is pristine, and his lush green lawn looks like he cuts each individual blade with a scissors to ensure uniformity. He's *that* guy.

He's got his serious face on while I'm probably sporting a look that says: *Spit it out and then be on your way.* I've got a feisty little girl trying to wiggle her way out of my hold while screaming, "Put me down!" so I'm running low on patience at the moment.

"I wasn't going to say anything, but this is the third night in a row." *What the hell is he talking about?* I take a step closer to the door to look around my property, to see that my garbage cans are put away and nothing's amiss. "That car that's always parked outside of your house?" He's barely able to hide his distaste when he says the word car, so I automatically know he's referring to Skylar's rusty old ride.

"What about it?"

"It's been parked at the end of the street for the past three nights in a row." When I don't respond right away he gets testy. "Last night I walked down to check if it was still there at midnight and there was someone *sleeping* in the backseat! We're not running a homeless shelter on the block now, are we, Leo?"

What a dick. "Not that I know of, Rob." Shaking my head, I add, "Go home, I'll look into it."

I don't trust that my nosy neighbor *will* go home, though. In fact, I'm kind of shocked that he hasn't just gone ahead and called the police already.

What to do? I think about bringing Libs along with me, but I'm not really sure what it is that I'm dealing with. Instead I walk her out to the deck and commit the worst parenting crime imaginable: giving in.

"Max, can you watch her for a second?"

"We've got her," Lexi offers, but when she opens her arms, Libby snubs her and goes to take Max's hand.

"Do *not* go near the pool, Olivia. I'll be right back."

"Everything all right?" Max asks.

I nod. "Be back in five."

I can see Skylar's car at the top of the hill. She's taken care to park it under a tree and away from any streetlights. She wants to stay out of sight.

What the hell is going on?

The inside of the car is illuminated from the glow her phone is giving off. She doesn't see me approaching so she startles when I tap on the window.

She takes a deep breath and then starts the car so she can lower the window. She's back to cool as a cucumber Skylar, but now it's not too hard to see past the mask she wears.

"Hey." She says it like there's nothing peculiar about this situation, as if camping out in her car is no biggie.

I make an effort to be quiet and gentle when I ask, "What are you doing?"

"Just reading," she says before lowering her head, and I can tell from her breathing and the way her shoulders move up and down that she's crying.

"Hey, hey..." I go to the other side of the car and get into the passenger seat. "Tell me what's going on." She doesn't answer, so I reach over to touch her cheek, careful and slow, and turn her to face me. "You can talk to me."

It takes her a few seconds and a few shaky breaths before she says anything. "I rented a summer sublet. I didn't know the girl personally...It was like a friend of a friend of a friend thing. The place is a dump. I mean, I knew that from the outset, but there are people coming and going all day and all night. It's like a twenty-four-hour house party. And the people are..."

"What?"

"I don't know...Older? Weird? Sketchy is the word I'd use, I guess."

"So you haven't been sleeping there?"

"I did the first couple of nights, but I was awake most of the time. My bedroom is on the first floor, so it's not like I can escape the noise. And then some guy, a friend of Holly's boyfriend came knocking on my door the last night I was there. I met him the day before I drove home when I went to drop off the rent." She lowers her head. "Let's just say I knew from that first impression that I shouldn't open my door."

"Are you fucking kidding me?"

"It's not as bad as I'm making it sound."

"That's bullshit."

"Leo..."

"Drive to the house."

"No!"

"I mean *my* house. You're staying there tonight and then we'll get your situation sorted out tomorrow."

"I don't need—"

"Stop." I have no patience for her Miss Independence routine right now. "Sometimes you *do* need help, Sky. We all do. Now *please*, let's go. Olivia's still awake and she's acting like a maniac. I have to get her to bed."

Her eyes nearly bug out of her head as she puts the car into drive. "You left her there alone?"

"No, Max is there."

Shit...Max and a few other people.

Chapter Thirty-Two

SKYLAR

Wetting my pants in third grade when the substitute teacher wouldn't let me use the bathroom? Getting caught by my pastor trying to buy cigarettes when I was fifteen? Filing a police report on my father with more than a few of my neighbors working in the precinct? Not one of those incidents compares to this.

I am mortified.

I feel like I'm going to be sick following Leo into the house. He fixes me with a look I can't read as he ushers me inside and then tosses my bag behind the couch.

That duffel bag, the one that now holds all my worldly possessions, made a pretty decent body pillow this week. For a moment he stares at the spot where it lands with a thump before turning back to me.

I don't want to face him, don't want to face Max, and I don't want to see Olivia for fear that I'll upset her once she sees the state I'm in.

"Hi!"

Instead I'm greeted by a girl who looks to be around my age. Long blonde hair, glowing skin, stylishly dressed in a snug cropped sweater over high-waisted shorts. I look down to the floor, mentally comparing my tear-stained face and bargain-bin clothing to hers, only to see the gold Tory Burch emblem on her sandals and her shiny red pedicure.

"Um, Skylar, this is Lexi. She came by with Max and his girlfriend."

Lexi the lawyer. Right.

"Skylar?" Her smile is over the top enthusiastic. I'm more hurt than confused, but still, I am wondering why she's looking at me like we're long lost friends or something. "You're Olivia's babysitter!"

I bite my lip and nod, still trying to absorb the impact from this blow.

"She *adores* you."

Lexi is putting out the whole *I'm looking to make friends* vibe, but there's a condescending bite to the way she delivers her words. Or maybe it's the look in her eyes. Or—deep breath —maybe she *is* being nice and I'm just being a sore loser and a bitch.

Leo looks hella uncomfortable. He opens his mouth to say something right as Olivia lets out a high-pitched wail. I start walking in the direction of the back door but Leo stops me. "I've got her." Glancing in Lexi's direction and then back to me he says, "Wait here," like it's an order.

He's walking back through the kitchen a moment later with a screaming Olivia over his shoulder, and her shrill cries only get louder when she catches sight of me. "Skylar!"

"It's all right, sweetie. Get some sleep and I'll see you in the morning."

"Noooo!" she protests, the sound echoing off the walls and then finally fading as he closes the upstairs bathroom door behind them.

"You look like you've had a rough night." Lexi is leaning a hip against the kitchen counter, studying me. She takes a sip from her bottle and then snaps out of it, giggling and shaking her head like she's just had some epiphany. "I'm sorry. Do you want a beer?" She opens the refrigerator like she's familiar with this kitchen, like she's a frequent guest. Turning back to me, she smiles when she asks, "Wait, are you even legal?"

"Is there some reason you're talking to me like I'm a child?"

"Sorry, I didn't mean anything by it." *Sure you didn't.* "I just figured you're the babysitter, so you know...Anyway," she chirps, "how old *are* you?"

"Same age as you, I'm guessing. Maybe a year younger. Did you just finish your first year of law school or what?"

"How do you know I'm in law school?"

"Leo told me about your date. He said you were a lawyer, but I think he got that part wrong. You don't look old enough."

She takes the beer she was planning to give me and opens it for herself. "I'm going into my second year." She smiles and breathes in deep before asking, "He told you about our date?" and without waiting for an answer she adds, "That's interesting."

I smile. "Not according to him."

And I hate myself in that moment. Hate that I'm being unkind to a stranger who's never truly wronged me. Hate that I am so envious of this girl. But tonight has been an absolute clusterfuck, and walking into *this*? A cozy double date? Maybe I should be grateful to this girl instead of hating on her. Maybe this will serve as the final slap in the face that I sorely need.

Max and his babe join us in the kitchen. Max looks curious and downright wary when he greets me. "Skylar...Everything all right?"

"Peachy." I just don't have it in me to be civil to anyone right now.

The other one holds out her hand. "I'm Nadia."

And I proceed to shake it like we're in a business meeting. "I'm Skylar."

Can this night get any more absurd?

I want to kill Leo right now for basically walking me into this nightmare. I'm shifting on my feet, feeling like a fool and dressed like I'm about to play hopscotch with Libs, while surrounded by two girls who are dressed for sex—I mean success—and basically look like they have their shit together.

I want out of here. I look to the spot on the counter where I usually drop my car keys and see that they're gone. *I'm going to kill him.*

It's like a four-way stare down for what feels like an eternity until Leo comes back. I shoot him a look that's meant to be interpreted as: *I'd like to claw your eyes out right now.*

"She finally went down?"

He answers Max, "Yeah, she's good," while his eyes stay fixed on me. And he has the nerve to look as pissed off as I do.

That's right, I forgot. I ruined his date, didn't I? Skylar Perillo, cockblocker extraordinaire. That's me.

My attention turns to Nadia when she pipes up and says, "They say parenting is the hardest job in the world."

To which Lexi lends her expert commentary, "But it's the most rewarding, too."

All eyes are on me now.

Jeez, did I just snort or something? Laugh out loud at that ridiculous scripted nonsense? I'm thinking maybe I did.

Oops.

"I'm heading out." I open my palm because I'm pretty sure Leo took my keys off the counter and pocketed them so I wouldn't run. "I can handle that situation on my own. Enjoy your night."

I'd rather sleep outdoors naked in February than subject myself to one more second of this.

He shakes his head and grabs hold of my wrist. "You're not going anywhere." Looking to Max he says, "Thanks for stopping in but I need to call it a night. Want me to call a car service for you guys?"

"No need. Nadia's taking one for the team tonight."

She raises her glass. "I switched to water a while ago."

I stand there like an unwanted stepchild as the small talk goes on, complete with Max suggesting the four of them grab dinner one night next week.

Leo is corralling them out the door when Lexi turns to him and says, "Thanks for having me." She leans in and kisses his cheek, and while it doesn't look like he was expecting it, I notice he doesn't pull away either. She glances at me before smiling at Leo. "Next time I'm hoping we'll have more time to talk."

He doesn't respond directly, just says, "Have a good night," as he's closing the door.

Leo turns and leans back against the door. He's pinching the bridge of his nose, asking God for patience or looking for a Hail Mary, for the best way to pave over this irreparable stretch of road.

I don't want the *sorry* that's coming, the one that's sitting on the tip of his tongue right now. I don't want his cheap excuses.

Why do I even want him? That's what I'm asking myself as

I grab a beer from the refrigerator. *Really, why would I want a guy like Leo?* I open the same drawer Lexi did a few minutes ago and fish out the bottle opener. *Yeah, she even knows where he keeps the kitchen utensils.*

I sit down, take a long pull from the bottle and wipe my mouth with the back of my hand. I don't care about table manners right now. I don't care what I look like or what he thinks of me. In fact, I hope my life choices, my background, and everything that I am disgust and repel him.

He goes to speak but I stop him. "Go to bed, Leo." A full minute passes with him standing his ground, so I change tack and ask him nicely, because seriously, I'm about ten seconds away from crying and beating on his chest the same way Olivia was before. "Please, I can't do this right now." My words come out wobbly and choked. I turn and give him my back knowing the tears are coming with or without my permission. I take another sip of my beer, then another.

I rest my head on the kitchen table to hide my face. I hear him fill a glass from the tap and then put it on the table next to me. He's close, I can sense it, and just the proximity of him hurts.

When he moves closer, rests his hand on my shoulder and squeezes, I can't help but break down. And I know without looking in the mirror that it's an ugly cry. One where your body shakes, your nose runs and your eyes swell. He keeps rubbing his hand over my shoulders and my back. I want him to stop but I don't want him to.

A good five minutes must pass before I stop crying, before I notice the dishtowel he laid on the table and use it to wipe my face. I think he's gone, that he did what I asked and left me, but then I see him in the living room making up the couch with a sheet and a blanket.

"I can't stay here."

Without looking my way, he answers back, "Yeah...You can."

I watch him walk back upstairs. I always watch, always take note of the way his large frame fills that narrow space. But tonight his shoulders are slumped in defeat.

He pauses on the stairs but doesn't turn around when he says, "Get a good night's sleep, Sky, and please don't run off. We'll talk in the morning."

Please don't run off.

As if I have anywhere to go.

I wait until I hear his bedroom door close before I make my way over to the couch and put my head down on the pillow he laid out for me. I nestle into it and breathe it in even though it hurts.

It smells like him.

Chapter Thirty-Three

LEO

"Sky is downstairs sleeping on the couch. We have to be super quiet so we don't wake her up."

"Why?"

"Because she doesn't feel good. She needs to sleep."

Olivia's eyes go wide. "She's sick?"

"She just needs to get a good rest." I prod her along as I dress her. "Let's go. Maureen is having you over for pancakes while I get some work done, and then you can come back and see Sky after she wakes up."

She side-eyes me, already knows when she's being fed a line of bull and she hasn't even turned five. It's scary.

"Chocolate chip pancakes?"

"Knowing Maureen, it'll be chocolate chip pancakes with some licorice bites and gummy worms thrown in for good measure."

"Eww, that sounds yucky."

"Yeah, that does sound gross."

I give Olivia one more *shh* before picking her up, opening her bedroom door and tip toeing down the stairs. Skylar shifts, rolls over in that tight space, but thankfully she doesn't wake up.

I drop Olivia off and then head right back. I was kind of shocked to see that Sky was still here when I woke up at four and peeked downstairs. I don't want to give her a chance to run. We've been circling around this same bullshit for weeks now, and I'm pretty sure that if she leaves now, I won't ever get her back.

I've only been gone for a few minutes, five tops, but the couch is empty with the sheet, blanket and pillow stacked in a neat pile next to it on the floor. I let out a relieved breath when I hear the water turn on upstairs and then the shower.

She stops halfway down the stairs and tenses when she sees me in the kitchen making breakfast a few minutes later.

"Did you get a good sleep?"

I busy myself with what's on the stove, stealing one quick glance over. Before she can turn away I catch sight of her face, see her puffy eyes, the mottled red of her usually perfect skin.

"Slept like the dead. Thanks."

When I see her stuffing her clothes from the night before back into her bag and zipping it up, I turn the burner off. Breakfast can wait.

Gesturing to her bag, I ask, "Did you take everything from the apartment?"

"All of my clothes. I left some of my books, maybe a few pairs of shoes. I'll go back and get them after I find another place." She pauses then adds, "I have an appointment with a realtor this afternoon."

"I'll take you to get your stuff now."

I choose not to call her out on the lie. There's no realtor

showing her apartments today. No one is leasing her an apartment for the six weeks she has left until she moves back into her free campus housing.

"I'll go there myself."

"No." She turns, startled by my tone. "I'm taking you and we're getting back every cent you paid in rent right now."

I'm expecting her usual, for her to fight me back, or in the very least, to call me a grump and tell me to kiss off. But she does none of that. She nods her head, looking so damn tired and defeated, then asks me to wait while she puts on some make-up. I'm confused for a second because she never wears much on her face, but then realize she wants to hide the fact that she's probably been up crying half the night.

When we pull up outside she says, "Wait here."

"I don't feel comfortable with that." The place is an absolute disgrace. An eyesore on a block where maybe the houses aren't upscale, but it's obvious that the neighbors are house proud. I already hate this girl Holly. "I won't make a scene. I promise."

Again, no words of protest. She lets herself out of the car and I follow, kicking trash out of my way as I take the stairs up to the porch. She doesn't even need a key to open the front door. Great, anyone can just walk right in.

There's a guy sleeping on the couch, complete with one hand shoved inside his boxers, and a girl sprawled out on a recliner wearing an oversized shirt with nothing on underneath. I know this because she's sleeping on her side and one entire ass cheek is exposed. Half-empty takeout containers, beer bottles and bongs litter every surface, and the place smells like weed mixed with sweat.

"No air conditioning?"

Sky turns to me. "He's a mechanic *and* a comedian."

She goes to the back room and opens the door. I follow and watch, dumbfounded as she starts stacking her books into a milk crate, oblivious to the guy who's taken up residence on her bed.

I kick the mattress. "Get up, asshole."

Sky shoots me a wide-eyed warning. "Leo!"

"What does this guy think he's doing crashing on your bed?"

I kick *him* this time and he wakes with a start. "What the fuck, man?"

"Get up and get out." I hear voices in the main room after he stumbles out, and can't help but call after him, "Does anyone wear clothes in this goddamn flophouse?"

I take the pink sheets off the mattress, wrapping all the bedding up with it, and then check on Skylar to see that she's packing the last of her things into another crate.

"What are you doing?" some snotty bitch calls from the doorway.

"Are you Holly?" Skylar digs her nails into my forearm but I'm not having it. When the girl nods, I tell her, "Skylar's moving out and *you* are returning every cent she paid you in rent right now. Cash or Venmo, your choice."

"Like hell I am."

"You might have given me a heads up, Holly. I haven't been here in days because you have people coming in and out of here all the time. Maybe you could have told me about your boyfriend's side hustle before I handed you a thousand dollars." Sky walks right up to her. "So you heard the man... Walk your skinny ass upstairs right now and get my money."

I can see the *fuck you* forming on Holly's lips when a familiar face pokes his head into the room. "What's up?" His eyes go wide. "Hey, Mr. Hale. Uh, what are you doing here?"

"Helping Sky move out and getting her money back."

"Oh, that's cool. It didn't work out?"

"No." Sky glares at him. "It didn't work out. Now tell your babe to go get my money."

He gestures for his girl to go upstairs and follow orders. "Are you kidding me right now? She paid the rent and there's no fucking refund policy."

"Get the money, Holly." He raises his voice and clamps a hand down on her shoulder. "Now."

A minute later we're walking back to the car with Greg following after us carrying the last of Skylar's things. Once everything is in the trunk I turn to him when he says, "I'll see you in a few weeks, Mr. Hale."

"I might have to rethink that." I look around the property and then back to him. "I don't like your act, don't like your girlfriend, and I don't want anyone on my team who treats his neighbors the way you do. This is a fucking disgrace. Clean this shit up, and then maybe we'll talk."

Yes, I've become *that* guy.

We both start laughing once we pull away from the curb.

"*Clean this shit up*?" She pretty much snorts and then says, "I can overlook the fact that you're a drug dealer, but the broken front door and the poor landscaping? Deal breaker."

"Do we have concrete proof that he's dealing? Doesn't matter because he's off my research team anyway."

She winces. "Yeah? I feel kind of guilty even though I know I shouldn't."

"This is a decent street and he's got no respect for the effort his neighbors put in to making it nice. Lack of respect and poor judgement, those are the deal breakers."

"Poor judgement?"

"Holly."

She nods. "I wish I snapped a picture of her face as she handed over that cash."

We share another laugh but then the air between us grows heavy again. I'm sure she feels it too because she starts grasping at straws, looking to distract and lighten the mood. "You didn't need to take the bedding. I don't think there's enough bleach in the world to sanitize it. He was crashing on my sheets buck naked. It's beyond gross."

"They'll be fine once they're run through the wash. No need to throw out perfectly good stuff."

She nods, bites her lip and looks out the window.

"I want you to stay in the pool house for the rest of the summer. Is that all right?"

"I told you I have an appointment—"

"With a realtor, I know. But think about it. You'd be paying a security deposit for what? A six-week rental? That's if you can even find a landlord who'll rent to you for only six weeks. I don't know much about real estate, but I'd say that's unlikely."

"It won't work. I'd be in the way."

We pull up outside the house and I turn to face her. "I'm just going to the say this so we can clear the air—"

She unclips her seat belt and gets out of the car while I'm mid-sentence. It's the grown-up version of covering your ears while screaming, I can't *hear* you!

I notice she doesn't take anything from the trunk before heading inside. I already know how she's going to play this, and I'm so grateful that Olivia is still across the street with Maureen right now because I'm about to blow.

When I follow her inside, she acts like she's scrolling through her messages. Like the imaginary real estate agent is blowing up her phone, wondering why she's missed all those apartment showings they had lined up for today.

I'm sure she knows I've been standing in place, arms crossed, just watching her for the past few minutes. She's strategizing, working it out, trying to solve this unsolvable problem on her own.

Her eyes are still glued to her phone when she finally speaks. "You'll say it's no problem, that I won't be in the way, but I will." She talks right over me, stopping me when I go to protest. "You're allowed a social life, Leo. We said we were going back to where we were. I've done that. I'm fine, so don't go thinking you have to explain last night away. Lexi seems all right, not that my opinion matters, but if you like her company and she makes you happy then I'm happy for you." She stops rambling for a nanosecond to take a breath before adding, "I'm glad you're putting yourself out there."

"Putting myself out there?"

Her eyes are soft when she finally looks to me. "It's been nearly four years since your wife passed away. Again, it's not my business, but you're young and you're a good person. You deserve to be happy."

"Yeah, you keep saying that."

"So that's why I don't think the pool house is a good idea." She shrugs and give me a pasted-on smile. "You should be able to entertain guests. How are you going to do that if I'm always around?"

"Could you please stop talking for a minute?"

"I just don't see—"

"Shut up!"

And she does just that. I may be a grumpy ass sometimes, but I've never raised my voice or spoken to her this way before.

And I probably look like a lunatic to boot. I can feel the vein in my neck ticking and my hands are fisted in my hair.

"Do you have any idea what it was like to find you in that car last night? To know you were in trouble and you didn't feel like you could come to me…That you couldn't trust me?"

"I trust you. It's not that."

"You put yourself in danger…The past three nights and every night you slept in that house with those assholes. I still can't believe you'd do something so stupid."

"I'm not listening to this." Going for the door, she says, "I'm not your kid, Leo, and you're not my daddy. Got it? I don't need anything from you."

I grab the doorknob at the same time she does. "So quick to run, aren't you? You keep trying to show me you're a woman but you're running away like a child." She tries to free her hand but I've got it trapped underneath mine. "You had your chance to talk. It's my turn now."

"Let me go."

"Not happening." I don't release her hand but I loosen my hold and make an effort to calm my voice. "You don't know how I felt last night so I'm going to tell you and I want you to listen." Her face is red, her expression is hard, but at least she's not fighting me. "I felt sick to my stomach walking up that hill to your car…Felt like I'd failed you. And then when we came back here, knowing you were going to read it all wrong, I wanted to put my fist through the wall." I tighten my hold on her hand again so she hears what I'm about to say. "I didn't invite them over, they just showed up. I didn't want her here. I barely know her."

"Why are you telling me this?"

"Because you think you know what I need and what's best for me when you don't know shit. Max, my parents…Even

Maureen says that crap all the time about moving on and putting myself out there, but to hear it from your lips?"

She lowers her head. "I meant it when I said you deserve to be happy."

"You think I don't want that for myself? You think I don't know what would make me happy? The *person* who would make me happy? I don't hold back because you work for me, and it's not that line I fed you about being too young. And please forget what I just said to you about acting stupid." I take my free hand and raise her chin. "You've been through so much, too much. But you just push through, paste a smile on your face and take care of everyone around you because that's just who you are. I think you're wiser, more compassionate and more responsible than most people twice your age."

"But you still—"

I shake my head, willing her to stop. "I want." And now it's me who has to look away. "Those words play on repeat whenever I look at you, whenever I think about you. I want."

"You want me." It comes out breathless.

"You know I do." I release her hand and step back. "And you think you want this too, so that's why I have to keep reminding myself that you *are* young. I won't take from you, and whether you agree with me or not, that's what I'd be doing."

"You think you'd be taking away my future or something? Taking away my choices?" She copies what I just did, takes my chin and forces me to look at her. "You can't take anything from me, Leo. You can't take anything that I won't give you."

She moves her hand from my chin to my cheek. "Life is short. We both know that better than anyone. So keep listening to that voice in your head that says *I want,* and stop listening to the one that lists all the reasons why you shouldn't."

Chapter Thirty-Four

SKYLAR

My head is spinning as I head over to Maureen's to get Olivia. I offered, used it as an excuse to clear my head and process everything that just passed between us.

Staring out Maureen's front window as she puts on some tea, I'm wondering where we can possibly go from here.

Leo comes outside and starts unloading the trunk that's still full of my things. He bypasses the front door and heads towards the backyard, so I take it that he's moving me into the pool house with or without my consent.

I want.

Leo Hale wants me. And I want him. But what now?

"No sugar, Sky?"

"Just milk. Thanks."

She gestures for me to come to the table and then fixes me with a look. "So what's the story?"

I sip my tea to buy some time even though it's scalding hot. "The story?"

Maureen shoots me a side eye before walking back into the kitchen to get some cookies out of the refrigerator.

"My mother always kept cookies in the fridge."

"Ice cold cookies with hot tea. Your momma is a smart woman."

"Was a smart woman."

"I'm sorry, Skylar. How long ago?"

"Thanks. It'll be a year next week."

She blows on her tea. "I lost my mother young, too." She reaches across the table to squeeze my hand. "It's hard."

"Some days it feels like it doesn't hurt as bad anymore, and then—"

"*Bam*! Some days it hits you."

"Exactly."

"Today one of those days?"

"Kind of."

Maureen looks over to where Olivia is sitting on the couch and sees that she's still into her movie. "Are you sure your mood doesn't have anything to do with our friend across the street?"

I shrug and look away. Don't have the energy to deny it anymore.

"He's just about the best young man I know." Now she's got my attention, because Maureen doesn't dish out accolades very often. "My two sons together don't make one half of the man he is, and that's something I hate to admit."

She looks out the window to see him hauling my bedding into the garage, probably on his way to the mudroom where the washer and dryer are.

"That one he married," she whispers, "was terrible to him. I'd see him drive off for work in the morning only to see her letting some other fella in not an hour later. Big pregnant belly and she was still at it." She nods in response to the open-mouthed stare I'm probably sporting. "And after the baby came she got worse. I had to let myself in a few times when I could hear Olivia screaming from across the street." She shakes her head in disgust. "On the couch passed out drunk at noon, the baby upstairs laying in a dirty diaper. I finally told Leo I'd have to call child services if he didn't do something about her."

"What did he say to that?"

"Poor thing. He was maybe twenty-five? He started working from home a lot more and I volunteered to watch Olivia whenever he needed me." She sips at her tea. "And then Carrie died soon after. Left him with a baby to raise and a scandal to deal with."

"What do you mean?"

"The man who was driving the car when Carrie was killed went on trial for manslaughter. From what I understand he had more than just alcohol in his system. I'm sure she did too but they don't speak ill of the dead." Maureen rolls her eyes because she'd think nothing of speaking ill of anyone living or dead if they deserved it. "Well, stand-up guy that he was, the man gave an interview to a reporter and claimed he was the real victim in all this." She lets out a cheerless laugh. "Claimed he was Olivia's father and mental anguish or some other BS drove him to abuse drugs and alcohol."

"Oh my God," I whisper.

She nods. "Yep. So here's Leo, trying to raise an infant all by himself and showing up to court nearly every day of the trial...For what reason I'll never understand. Knowing Carrie the way *I* did, I didn't care if the guy hung or got off scot free, but Leo's more honorable than I am. Apparently that piece of trash gave some half-assed apology statement in which he said that he hoped to have a relationship with his daughter when he got out of prison someday. Leo got the paternity test, though. Proved Olivia was his. But can you imagine going through that ordeal?"

"No. I can't."

She takes our cups to the sink, peeking her head back in to look at Olivia when she says, "So be easy on him, ok?"

I nod and then force a smile. "Ready to go, Libs?"

"Can we go in the pool?"

"Yeah, it's hot. A swim sounds like a great idea."

Holding my hand as we cross the street, Olivia looks up at me and says, "Daddy is mad at me."

"Why do you think he's mad?"

She tugs on my hand so I'll look down at her. Making a scowling face she says, "He looked like this before."

I laugh to lighten the mood. "He looks grumpy lots of times. Doesn't mean he's mad at you."

"He is. I said something mean."

"Hmm...When I say something that's not nice, I apologize. I'm sure your dad will understand. We all get cranky and say things we don't mean sometimes."

"I told him I was gonna run away from home."

I can't help but wince. "Ooh, Libs. That would make your father sad more than anything else. Did you mean it? Do you want to run away?"

"No."

"So when you get a chance later on, tell him you're sorry and that you didn't mean it. Your dad will always forgive you because he loves you more than anything."

This seems to appease her. "I'm gonna make him a picture." She looks up to me again. "And then we go in the pool?"

"I think he'd really like that, and sure, we'll swim after."

It's been less than half an hour, but when I find him out in the pool house he already has a mattress set up, my crate of books and my bag are in the corner, and he's rolling an old garment rack from the garage into place. He doesn't look my way but knows I'm here.

"I hope this is all right. I don't want to force your hand or anything, but short of getting some totally overpriced rental, I figured this is the best option."

"Leo, your pool house is nicer than the house I grew up in. Probably the same size, too." Trying to ease the tension, I shrug and add, "I guess it'll do."

The pool house looks like something out of a high-end home design magazine. French doors open out onto a deck with comfy couches and lounge chairs, and there's a large screen television in case you want to catch a movie or watch a game outdoors. I wasn't joking, either—it's around the same size as our small ranch house.

"And you're ok...With everything?"

"Yeah. We'll be fine."

I don't know what that means exactly and I'm sure he doesn't either. We've put ourselves into some weird sort of limbo, or a purgatory of some kind.

He wants me but won't do anything about it. I want him but I get the feeling that if I push this thing between us that I might lose him. Patience is a virtue I'm sorely lacking in, but I can do this.

For Leo I'd wait a lifetime.

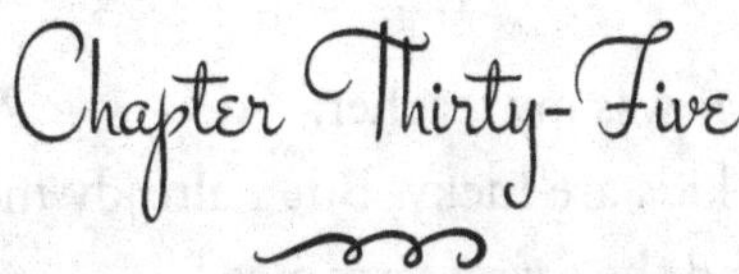

Chapter Thirty-Five

LEO

"Is my big girl ready for her first day of kindergarten?"

She's checking herself out in the mirror, turning back and forth to watch as the pleats in her skirt move and twist with the movement. "Is Clementine in my class?"

"That's one of the fun things about the first day of school. You get to meet your new teacher and you find out which kids are in your class. And remember, there are only two kindergarten classes so even if Clementine is in the other class you'll still see her at lunch and recess."

"What's recess?"

"It's when you get to run around and play in the schoolyard after lunch. It's the best."

"Is Skylar picking me up today? I want her to see my outfit."

Olivia looks like the character from the Madeline books, with her yellow pleated dress and the red bow in her hair.

Skylar picked it out for her and gave it to her as a surprise last week before she left to go visit her sister.

"No, baby. It's the first day of school for Skylar today, too. And your first day is special so I want to be there to pick you up."

"I wish Skylar was my teacher."

"Yep, those kids are lucky. But I already met your teacher, Miss Winters, and she's very, very nice."

Olivia shrugs her shoulders as if to say, *We'll see about that.* Yeah, no one compares to Skylar in my daughter's eyes.

"Sky is picking you up on Tuesdays and Thursdays, so she'll be there tomorrow after school."

"I wish she still lived at home with us."

So do I.

"She's back at school now, Libs. And this is her last year so she's super busy. She's teaching three days a week and then has classes on the other days." I want to add, *Believe me, no one's more disappointed about the living arrangements than I am.*

We've been doing a good job of keeping things quasi platonic. Skylar stayed the rest of the summer in the pool house and I think it turned out better than either one of us expected. We fell into a routine, kept our hands off one another for the most part, and got to know one another a lot better.

Sky and Olivia would already be down in the kitchen making breakfast together by the time I got out of bed, and the sight of them side by side, talking and laughing, was the best thing to wake up to. Some days I'd skip going to the shop and work from home just so I could be around them. She kept Olivia busy all summer taking her to museums, to the zoo, to community theater shows and hosting her little friends at our pool a few times. Sky also took her down to see her sister's family and stayed overnight there with her twice.

Olivia is a happy kid by nature, but I don't think I've ever seen her as bubbly as she's been since Skylar's been in the picture.

I try not to let myself go there, but this summer was like playing house. With the exception of taking in two night games with the guys to cheer my Pirates on over the Reds, I didn't do a whole lot. Nights spent grilling in the backyard, going for ice cream, or watching a movie on the outdoor screen were some of the best times I've ever had.

But I'd remind myself that while I'm pushing thirty, Skylar isn't, so I'd nudge her to go out and meet up with her friends. Pilar and Devon, two of her dance buddies, were the only ones who stayed in town for the summer, but Sky preferred to have them over here to hang out rather than meet up with them when they were going out to the bars or clubs.

"It's not really my scene," she'd say, and I came to realize that she wasn't bullshitting me, it just wasn't.

Sky likes to stay busy and she's always on the move, but she likes simple things like cooking, reading a book by the pool and spending time with her family.

Every once in a while she'd have a glass of wine or a beer with me after dinner, but she'd turn the offer down more times than she said yes, and she always stopped at one.

I stopped at one, too. Having her around all the time was great, but I'm not going to lie, it was a challenge. Skylar hugging my daughter close, Skylar kissing Olivia's head every time she snapped her into her booster seat, Skylar dancing in the kitchen when she thought no one was watching, and Skylar out by the pool alone at night just staring at the night sky—I was fighting every day against everything I wanted.

It's been the hottest August on record, and while our central air conditioning keeps the house nice and comfortable, the pool house isn't hooked up to it. There are a few ceiling fans to cool the space, but that's it. I told her to take the guest room next to Olivia's in the main house more times than I could count, but she refused every time.

So along with all the other things I've had to contend with this summer, I've been stuck with a visual of Skylar out in that pool house with her sweat-slicked skin, twisting and then kicking off the sheets.

I know what she wants. Know she's been trying her best to ignore this undeniable attraction and not act on those impulses, same as me. And in this case I'm thankful that trying your best doesn't always guarantee success.

The one night we did go and cross that line, it was Skylar's doing.

I shake myself out of that memory, same as I've done more times than I can count over the past few days.

From the rearview mirror I see Olivia staring out her window looking unsettled. "What's on your mind, baby girl?"

"Sky said she's nervous for school today."

"She did?"

Olivia fixes me with that look, the one that tells me I'm being thick. "Everyone is nervous for new things."

"Sky has no reason to be nervous. She's going to make a great teacher, don't you think?"

"Can I call her?"

"Um..." I check the clock on the dashboard. "She doesn't have to be in until eight-thirty, so yeah, you can give her a quick call."

I pull into a spot at Olivia's school and hand her the phone after hitting Sky's contact. I hear Sky answer a moment later with the enthusiastic greeting she always gives Libs that makes her feel special.

It's so damn cute when Olivia says, "Don't be nervous, ok?" that I have to stifle a laugh. And when Skylar ends the call telling Olivia to have the *best first day of kindergarten ever* and that she loves her, I swallow back the emotion.

She's said it to her hundreds of times, and while it used to make me uneasy, now it makes me feel content, fortunate—or maybe hopeful is a better way to describe it.

I still wrestle with whether or not getting involved with Skylar is a good idea. She can say whatever she wants, tell me I'm overthinking this and denying her something she's choosing, but the facts don't lie. I'm a parent, and getting involved with me is different from dating a man who's at the same stage in life that she's at.

But maybe it's because she's put it out there, or maybe it's because I'm selfish, but I just don't have it in me to hold back anymore.

I want.

And I'm ready to take.

SKYLAR

The ball is officially in Leo Hale's court.

The night before I left, I didn't suggest, didn't just put it out there. No, I left him no doubt. He knows how I feel and he knows what I want.

The next move is his.

He's contacted me over the past week, simple texts that would seem routine or mundane to anyone else, but I'm reading between the lines.

Olivia keeps making me show her next Saturday on the calendar. She's going to drive me nuts until you come back.

How are Garth and Sienna and the baby doing? Tell everyone me and Libs say hello.

It's quiet around here without you around.

I tell him to give Olivia hugs and kisses from me, tell him that James is getting so big and starting to babble a lot, and I remind him that Olivia's new lunch bag should be coming in the mail this week. But to that last text I reply: *I miss you, too.*

I don't have it in me to go slow anymore. I kind of said *screw it* last week, so there's no point in trying to go in reverse and be cautious now.

I've been flighty all week, daydreamy and smiling to myself. And while I'm enjoying this time with my sweet little nephew, and with Sienna and Garth, the truth is I'm itching to get back.

I want his hands on me the way they were last week. I want his kiss.

The look on his face was priceless. I saw the light turn on in the living room when he came back down from putting Olivia to bed, and I timed it so that he'd catch me lowering myself into the pool. I packed away those prim one-piece numbers I'd bought for the summer and slipped into one of my bikinis instead. Yeah, the one that shows more than a little bit of cheek.

"It's so hot tonight," I whispered when I turned to see him watching me.

"I told you to sleep in the house. You're always so damn stubborn."

"I'm fine sleeping out here."

"It's not dropping below ninety tonight," he said absently, eyes fixed on my body.

I ducked under and then came up in the shallow end so I was standing in waist-deep water. It wasn't fair, putting the goods on display like that, but I was looking to push him. Laying back into the water to float, I said, "It feels good in here."

He stood there saying nothing for a minute, just watching

as I floated and stared right back up at him. And just when I was starting to fear that he was going to turn around and go back inside, to reject me, Leo pushed his shorts down over his hips and let them drop to the deck.

I stood back up, chest-deep in the water now, and looked over every inch of him. *Is it me, do I make him like that?* I knew the answer to that question and it made me feel powerful.

"Come in," I said, and he obeyed.

When he got close, I slipped my arms around his neck and pressed into him, eager to feel him against me.

"Skylar."

This time he didn't speak my name like a warning. No, he wasn't fighting his conscience anymore. This time my name was whispered in reverence and laced with desire.

Leo lifted me and wrapped my legs around his waist before lowering his head. "You sure?"

I kissed him, licked the seam of his lips until he opened up for me and took over. A low moan rose from his chest as he crossed the pool to the steps, kissing me uninterrupted as he walked us up and out of the water and then laid me down on my bed in the pool house. Leo broke the kiss and stood back up, never taking his eyes off me as he pushed the snug, wet fabric of his boxers down his hips and thighs. I sat up, wanted to make sure his eyes stayed fixed on me as I undressed for him too. I watched his face as I undid the strings on my bikini top, heard him drag in a breath as I revealed myself to him. He didn't let me get to my bottoms. He pinned my hands above my head and laid me back as he continued to stare.

"Leo," I pleaded, but I didn't say anything more. He knew I wanted him, knew I wanted him to ease everything in me that ached.

"You're so beautiful, Sky. Everything about you is beautiful."

He lowered his head then, took one breast in his mouth, taking his time as he sucked and licked. I'm not sure what sounds I was making in the lust-drunk haze I was in, I just know that when I was on the verge of begging him to touch me, it's like he heard my silent plea. One hand moved from my other breast, across my stomach and down, slipping past the fabric of my bottoms and sinking right into me. It felt so good I could hardly catch my breath. And with the heavy weight of him pressing into my thigh and his mouth still teasing my breasts, it was sensory overload. With one hand fisted in his hair, I was a writhing, needy mess, calling out his name and begging for him to give me what I wanted.

"Come on, baby…That's it," he whispered, urging me on.

I read somewhere that the French word translates to *the little death*, and now I get it. My breaths came in shallow, my heartbeat raced, and the muscles pulsed where his hand still pressed against me. I've gotten there by myself before, but nothing compared to the way I felt when it was Leo's doing, live and in the flesh as opposed to my fantasies.

I nudged my bottoms down and then slid my hand between us. He was hard as stone but went back to kissing me gently, always in control and looking to put the brakes on us. "I'm not on anything," I whispered, and he answered back, "It's ok, I figured that."

"I'm sorry."

I said it more to myself than to him. Why the hell had I gone off the pill?

"Don't say that. I'm not sorry about anything."

"Do you have something?"

He kept laying kisses on my neck and shifting his sweat-slicked body against mine. "I don't need that tonight. Just keep touching me, your hand feels good."

But I still remembered how it used to be, how to get creative if you wanted it but weren't ready to go all the way.

I moved out from underneath his body and gestured for him to get on his back so I could straddle him. *Right here, Leo.* I willed him to keep his eyes locked on mine as I rocked my hips back and forth along his length without taking him in. *I'm about to blow your mind.*

He moaned when he gripped my hips with both hands, pulling me down to press against him as I kept up that slow agonizing pace. Back and forth, back and forth I moved, as Leo's eyes roamed from my face to my breasts, to where our bodies met and then back up again.

I could tell he was getting close when his fingers dug in and he took over, upping the pace. Head thrown back, he whispered my name like I was killing him when he came. And a minute later, when his breathing evened out and his heavy eyes opened back up to look at me, he pulled me down, wrapped me in his arms and said, "I cannot wait to be inside you someday."

I promised him, "Someday soon."

"Sky?" I'm confused for a second before I realize that, no, I'm not in the pool house, and that the voice calling my name belongs to Garth, not Leo. "I said the burgers will be ready soon. American or cheddar?"

When it comes to food lately, I could care less. It's like I've got a twenty-four-seven case of butterflies in my stomach and nourishment of the food and beverage variety is the last thing on my mind.

I'm picking at the seeds on the top of my bun when Garth asks, "Are you nervous about Monday or something?"

It takes me a moment to process what he means. "About school?"

He joins me at the picnic table. "Yeah...New job and all that."

"It's still only student teaching but I do want to make a great impression on the administration. I'd love to get offered a job in that school district next year."

Sienna looks up from nursing James. "So you're set on staying up near Pittsburgh?"

"Um...Nothing is decided. It's a long way off and who knows where I'll get hired."

Garth speaks around a mouthful of food. "You'd get hired here. Mr. Gibbons is still the principal at the elementary school."

I shrug and then look over to see Sienna watching me with a smile on her face. "What?" I ask her.

"Is it Leo who's got you this way?"

"What are you talking about?"

"Sitting there with a dreamy smile on your face and making plans for the future to be wherever he is."

It's too new to hope for a future with him, even though it's all I do. "I just don't know."

"Yeah," my sister smiles back, "you do."

LEO

Sky got back from Garth and Sienna's and moved straight into the dorms. I'm not going to lie, dropping her stuff off with Olivia that morning felt all sorts of awful.

My request for her to watch Olivia while I worked that next Saturday came out of nowhere. I really had nothing pressing to do, so I spent the morning daydreaming in the garage about how Skylar and I were going to take up right where we'd left off that night in the pool house.

I came back around dinnertime after running unnecessary errands with food and snacks for the barbecue I assumed we'd be having. Yeah, I had it all planned out: steaks on the grill, movie with Olivia, put Olivia to bed, some wine on the deck, a swim...

Truth be told, fantasizing about the post-swim activities had taken up most of my day, so I was surprised—and sorely disappointed—when she told us she was heading out with friends after dinner. Sky rolled her eyes when she said that Pilar wouldn't leave her alone, guilting her into a night out dancing.

Just the mention of Skylar dancing had my mind going back to the first night we didn't actually meet, and when I got a look at what she was wearing, I'll admit to feeling more than a little territorial. Same as that first time I laid eyes on her, Skylar's curves were on display and her dress revealed a whole lotta leg.

Olivia was mesmerized, of course, and started peppering Skylar with questions. When my daughter pressed to tag along, Skylar gave her a hug when she answered, "Sorry, Libs, you have to be at least twenty-one."

Now if *I* said that, there would still be three rounds of negotiation to get through, but when Skylar laid down the law it was a one-and-done situation. Maybe it's because she's so nice that Olivia doesn't even realize when she's being told no. *Hmm.*

"That's Mischa," she said when a horn sounded outside. Looking back to me with her hand on the doorknob, she smiled and winked when she added, "I hope tonight lives up to the last time I went to this club."

She winked, I told myself. That was a signal, right? Had to be. And she brought her clothes here to change into, which was odd, I reminded myself. She wanted me to see. The make-up, the heels...She planned it this way, didn't she?

Skylar had me questioning myself like a fourteen-year-old with a bad crush. A few minutes ago my hopes were dashed, but now I was downright giddy.

Maureen was in full busybody mode when I asked for a last-minute save, but I thanked the stars above when she agreed to come over after Olivia was tucked in for the night. I didn't even mind her twenty questions routine for once, knowing it was a small price to pay.

It was dark and deserted on that street, same as last time, and when the heavy steel door opened, it was an assault on the senses. Yeah, I still wasn't a fan of the loud, pumping base that rattled the walls and left my ears ringing, but when I caught sight of her on the dance floor, the music, the pulsing lights and the voices faded out.

Skylar was with her friends, smiling, arms up in the air and shaking her hips. Took my breath away. I looked around, dumbfounded for a second, wondering how every set of eyes in this place was not focused on her and her alone.

When the song changed, she watched as her four friends morphed into two couples swaying slowly in time to the music. I moved in, watching as Sky attempted to weave her way through the crowd, intercepting her right as she got to the edge of the dance floor.

"You like this?" I asked as I wrapped my arms around her from behind, attempting to recreate that scene from so long ago.

Her body stiffened for a moment, but then she looked down and ran her fingers over the inked skin of my forearm. "Yeah," she whispered on a raspy breath, "feels nice."

There was no eye contact, no words. Just her body pressed against mine, her back to my front, our hips rocking in time to the slow pulsing beat of the music. And just like the last time, she reached up and arched back, lacing her fingers at the nape of my neck.

"You feel so good," I murmured into her ear, and she responded with a sound that was low and full of longing. "Come with me," I said as I led us off the floor and down a dark hallway that led to a back bar.

She tugged on my hand when we were halfway there, and when I turned, she fisted my shirt in both hands and leaned in close as she ran her nose along the column of my neck. "Tell me your name," she said on a breathy exhale.

It took me a second to catch on to the game she was playing.

"No names," I said, shaking my head as I backed her against the wall, "but I'll give you what you want tonight."

And that kiss could have set an entire city block on fire. Lips and hands searching, teeth scraping—could have been five minutes or half an hour before we came up for air.

"I want you." The words came out in a torrent, more hungry for this woman now than I'd ever been for anyone in my life. As she teased her lips along my neck and my collarbone, I spilled every secret I had. "Wanted you for so long, since the first day I laid eyes on you." Grinding my body against hers for some relief, I wasn't even sure what was coming out of my mouth, but it was some version of: *I need it, Let me, I want to take you right now.*

I did want it right there and then, too. Wanted to drag her into a supply closet, the backseat of my car, anywhere. But this wasn't a fantasy, it was real life, and when I came to, I noticed a club security guy stopped in his tracks, staring at us with a dazed look in his eyes and an open mouth. Felt bad for the poor bastard, but we weren't putting on a live show for anyone.

"My car's out back," I told her. "Let's go home."

And the drive back was the best sort of torture, as Skylar kept up the ruse, telling me she never spoke to strangers, and never ever went home with random guys. All this talk as she grazed her fingernails across my chest and then down, down, down.

I parked ten feet past my driveway and eased the back gate

open without making a sound. Not that it mattered; Maureen listened to the television so loud we could hear the jarring *dun-dun* that signaled the start of *Law & Order* as we made our way across the backyard.

After a quick prayer that Olivia was still up in bed and not being subjected to a serial killer storyline, I tugged Skylar's hand as she went to enter the pool house. "No, in here."

In that moment, I was so glad I insisted on an outdoor shower during the renovations. The pool and the cabana are nice, don't get me wrong, but there's something about showering outdoors in the summertime that feels wild and untamed. I mentally put that on my *things to do with Skylar* list, which was just started last week but growing by the day.

Aside from the occasional sound of a car passing by in the distance, you couldn't hear much over the sound of our breathing. It was dark in that small space, but all you had to do was look up to see a small sliver of the moon doing its best to illuminate that end-of-summer sky.

"I'm ready," she said, looking me in the eye. I knew Skylar was on the pill now, but she read the hesitation in my expression. "Leo..." And with that plea, Skylar ended the game, nestling her head against my chest. "I want this, ok? And I don't want to wait any longer."

To prove her point, she unzipped her small purse and produced a condom, which she placed in my hand, and then turned her back to me as she hiked her dress up and over her hips. Her voice was a whispered plea when she said, "Now, Leo. Please, I need you."

"You are so beautiful, you know that?" Impatient, she pushed her ass back against me, reaching both of her hands back to ease me out of my pants. "And you're greedy," I teased.

The feel of her skin, the sounds she made as I swept my

fingers and lips over any spot I could get to in that cramped space—it was the best kind of torture and she was so worth the wait.

It had been a long time. So long I'd almost forgotten how alive desire makes you feel. There's nothing more natural in the world than two people wanting one another, and the anticipation—the primal joy coursing through every cell in my body—made me feel more alive than I had in years. I could have wept at the sound when she said my name, over and over and over, as I pushed into her again and again and again.

Coming down from it all, I couldn't help but wonder how I'd gotten so lucky, so blessed. Heaven was the only word that could come close.

Being with her was heaven.

Chapter Thirty-Eight

LEO

It's Friday and I still haven't told Olivia that I'm taking Skylar out for dinner tonight. I'm wrestling with whether or not I even should.

"Libs, there's something I want to run by you."

She looks up from her waffles and gives me her full attention. "What's up?"

"Maureen is coming over for a little while to watch you tonight."

"You going to play cards with Max?"

"Nope...I'm going out on a date tonight...With Skylar."

"Like Tracy and Link?"

She's into *Hairspray* now. Thanks to Skylar, I now have to listen to *Good Morning, Baltimore*, morning, noon and night.

But Olivia is smiling like a happy little loon right now, so I'll go with it. "Yep, I guess so."

"Are you gonna be Skylar's boyfriend?"

I'd like to say, *Yes, yes I am*, but I don't really know how this is going to play out.

"Libs, it's a little complicated. Real life isn't like the movies. I don't know if I'll be her boyfriend, but no matter what, she'll always be my friend and yours, too."

"But you like her?"

"Yeah, I do."

"Like she's a special person?"

I nod. "I think she's really special."

"Are you gonna hold her hand tonight?"

Here we go. "Hold her hand?"

"Yes! And you should give her a kiss goodnight. Then she'll be your girlfriend."

I should have kept my trap shut. "Olivia, don't—"

I'm about to tell her not to get her hopes up when she cuts me off. "It's ok, Daddy. She likes you too."

"And how do you know that?" I ask it as a joke even though I'm more than a little curious.

"She looks at you like Belle looks at the beast."

"That's a good thing?"

She nods as she takes another bite of her waffle. "Yep."

Skylar opens the door with wide eyes. "I thought you'd text me and I'd meet you downstairs."

"Is this ok?"

She laughs as she leads me into her room. "It's fine with *me*. I just know how you operate, so I figured you'd be having a minor panic attack picking your date up at her college dorm."

I scratch the back of my neck. "I was having a moment on the ride over, but I just kept telling myself that I'm not your professor and I don't work here. I'm an adult and you're an adult—"

"Deep breath, Leo."

"What I'm trying to say is that I'm over the age difference thing if you are."

"It was never an issue for me."

But I can't let it go that easily, so I press the issue over dinner.

We're at a brick oven place in Oakland that's close to campus where she meets Grace for dinner once or twice a month. She's been raving about their clam oreganata pie, which sounds awful, but she's convinced me that I need to try it.

The clientele is a mix of students, professors from Carnegie Mellon and Pitt, and young professionals.

My eyes keep drifting over to the corner where there's a table of six people who are obviously students, three guys and three girls.

"Remember when you asked me if I thought people were difficult to read?" I look back to her and watch as she takes a sip of her wine. "You specifically asked me if I thought it was hard to read men."

"Hmm?"

"You, Leo Hale, are very easy to read at the moment."

I swirl the wine around my glass, stalling before I take a sip. "How's that?"

"You keep looking at that group over there. They're around my age, give or take a year, and you're telling yourself that I should be with one of *those* guys instead of you. Am I right?"

"None of the guys on campus turn your head?"

"I've been asked out on a few dates—"

"I'm sure it's been more than a few."

She brushes my comment off and says, "It's hard to explain, but the things that seem important to most people my age just aren't important to me. I don't want to deal with drunk guys at frat socials and I don't want to drink my face off before football games at the tailgate parties. Maybe if I came here at eighteen as a naïve freshman things would be different, but that's not how my life has played out."

I think on that as the server comes over with our pie and Skylar slides a slice onto a plate for me and then does the same for herself.

She blows on the piping hot slice and then looks up to me. "You're awful quiet over there, so I'll answer that question you're not asking me. I won't look back on this time in my life and regret it."

"You can't guarantee that."

"You're right, there are no guarantees." She shakes her head. "I can't believe I'm about to use a gambling term here, but Leo, I'd bet the farm on this...On us."

And now I'm smiling because I can't help it. "And what's the over-under on me liking this pizza? It smells like garlic and ass."

She leans in and lowers her voice. "You smell like ass, you fool. And if you don't like this pizza then there's simply no hope for you." Biting into her slice, she lets out an orgasmic moan, drawing the attention of two guys sitting at a nearby table.

"Oh, you're gonna get it, Skylar."

She tips her head to the side, teasing me. "Promises, promises."

I take a bite of my pizza, and while I may not feel quite the same way about it that Skylar does, I have to admit that it's better than decent.

I nod. "It's better than I expected."

"Right?" She takes another bite and then says, "It's like the best of both worlds…Garlic bread and yummy baked clams."

"There's a place in New York that has the best baked clams. Not that I'm an aficionado like you are," I tease, "but it's been years and I still remember them."

"How many times have you been there?"

I shake my head as I actually try to come up with a number. "I don't even know…So many times that I couldn't say."

"Do you remember the name of the restaurant? I'll put it on my list for when I go back."

"It was after a long day of bar hopping around the Village. Thompson Street, maybe off Bleeker? I don't remember the name."

"I tried baked clams for the first time in New York. We ate at an Italian restaurant in the Theater District that you'd probably consider a tourist trap because you're a snob—"

"Am not!"

She talks right over me. "—but I loved it."

I'm quiet for a moment, not entirely sure if I should put this out there so soon. "I was thinking about surprising Olivia with a trip to New York for her birthday."

Skylar smiles and closes her eyes like she's lost in a good memory. "She would absolutely *love* that."

"It's coming up at the end of the month and there's a school holiday on that Monday, so I was thinking we could make a long weekend of it."

She takes another bite and nods as she chews. "I saw it on our district calendar…A religious holiday. It's either Rosh Hashanah or Yom Kippur, right?"

"I'm not sure which. So that works with your schedule? You'll come?"

"You want me to come with you?"

"I want you there, yeah."

She goes quiet, looks down into her lap for a moment before she meets my eyes with a soft smile. "Then I wouldn't miss it for the world."

Chapter Thirty-Nine

SKYLAR

"I don't think you can cram anymore tinsel onto that tree, Libs."

"Sure I can," she says as she tosses some more in the general vicinity of the tree, moving her arms like she's sprinkling fairy dust. "See?"

"I stand corrected. Here," I hand her one of the ornaments from the storage box, "let's start hanging these."

After hanging that first one she comes over to pick through the box herself. "Ooh, a snowman."

"I like that one. And look at this...Mickey Mouse in a Santa hat." I hand it to her so she can hang it and then start rummaging deep into the box. "Minnie must be around here somewhere."

Leo comes in with a paper bag. "I just remembered the ones from our trip. They were still in your luggage, Olivia."

She comes over and helps him to unwrap them from the tissue paper. The first one is a snow globe with the Empire

State Building standing tall amid the other skyscrapers, a Broadway sign, and a big apple inside. That was my corny pick, and Leo teased me unmercifully after I bought it from a street vendor.

"Hand it over," I order him with a phony frown, and then shake it and smile as the snow falls over that magical cityscape.

Then there's an oversized Olaf wearing a pink bedazzled scarf. Olivia takes it and says, "This one is my favorite," as she circles the tree looking for a prime location.

Leo unwraps the last one. He looks at the little figure in his hands and then looks back to me smiling.

"What is that?"

He holds it up to show me as Olivia comes back over. Her eyes go wide. "The hot dog man!"

And yes, it's a replica of one of those sidewalk hot dog carts, complete with the umbrella and a man dressed in an apron. "That's adorable! When did you get it?"

"While you two were busy bankrupting me in the American Girl store, I went into some cheesy tourist shop to kill some time."

Handing it over to Olivia, he says, "It was either that one or the Rockettes kick line. But I figured we'd get that next time...Maybe we'll catch the Christmas show at Rockefeller Center next year."

I waggle my eyebrows. "The Rockettes, huh?"

Leo pulls me onto his lap. "I like dancers."

When Libs comes over he pulls her in and starts tickling us both. We're laughing and breathless and screaming for him to stop when the three of us fall onto the rug in a heap.

I roll onto my back, still laughing, and Olivia settles into the crook of my arm. She has tinsel in her hair and her cheeks are bright red, and I'm sure I look the same.

When I look to Leo I see that he's sitting up again and watching us. It's hard to read his expression.

"What's up?"

"Huh?"

"You look like this," I tell him, contorting my face into a super serious pout.

Olivia jumps on the bandwagon, making the same face. "Yeah, Daddy, you look like a grump."

I raise an eyebrow and fix her with a look. "We said we're not using that word anymore, remember?"

Olivia gets up and brushes the pine needles and tinsel from her leggings, walking back over to admire the tree. So quietly that she thinks no one else can hear, she says, "But he does look like a grump sometimes."

She's right, but I don't like teasing Leo that way anymore. I've come to realize that his grumpy exterior can be a front for times when he's worried about Libby, about me, or on rare occasions, about work-related stuff. So no more making fun. The people in your life who love you are supposed to be there to make it better and to ease those worry lines.

Moving back onto his lap, I wrap my arms around his neck. "Is everything all right?"

"Better than all right. I'm happy."

"You looked worried or something for a minute there."

He lets out a soft laugh. "Grumpy dudes tend to do that. We worry whenever we're happy."

"You're waiting for the other shoe to drop, huh?"

"It's feels too good to be true, you know?"

"No." I shake my head before planting one soft kiss on his cheek. "This is how it's supposed to be, Leo. Trust in this."

"They're here!" Olivia runs over to us. "Quick, get the gate!"

We ordered a gate, outlet covers, and rubber bumpers to cover every sharp edge on the first floor in preparation for the arrival of the Messiah, otherwise known as my nephew, James.

"Ta-da!" Olivia calls out as Garth comes in carrying James's car seat with Sienna following behind. "We got a gate so James can't eat the tree!"

Sienna and I start cracking up at that one but Garth nods his head, all serious. "You're always thinking, Olivia. He'd make a meal out of that tinsel." They fist bump as he says, "Good job."

"Is James crawling yet?" she asks Sienna.

"He gets up on his hands and knees and rocks back and forth, so it should be soon. C'mere and give me a hug."

"You smell good," Olivia says as she nestles into Sienna's arms.

"I was baking goodies all morning so I should smell good!"

I peek into the containers Sienna set down on the table when she came in. "Apple pie with extra crust baked into the shape of a Christmas tree on top, cupcakes with reindeer faces, and sugar cookies in the shape of Santa hats." Shaking my head I look back to my sister. "Even if this stuff doesn't taste good you get an A for effort."

"As if." She scoffs. "I could win the Great American Bake-Off with that apple pie."

And with John Legend's *Bring Me Love* playing in the background, I start rocking from side to side and then break into a sexy little shimmy. "Don't know about a bake-off, but I'm pretty sure I can take you in a dance-off nowadays."

"Did you hear that, Olivia?" She comes next to where I'm standing in the kitchen and hip checks me off balance. "Thems fightin' words!"

"Yeah, thems fightin' words!" my little traitor says as she

comes over and takes Sienna's hand. And watching Olivia as she tries to imitate every single step my sister takes, I'm overcome with this feeling of goodness and love for every person in this house.

For a moment I think to myself that it's like Leo says, too good to be true, but it's really not.

This love? It's true.

I trust in this.

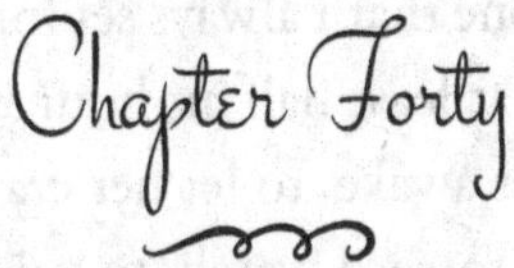

Chapter Forty

LEO

After dinner, lots of wine and way too much dessert, we get Olivia to bed and then get Garth and Sienna settled in the guest room with James.

Tipsy Skylar looks to me smiling. "Um, where am I sleeping tonight?"

We've been careful not to do anything that will confuse Olivia, but Skylar has stayed over at the house at least one night a week since she moved out after the summer. It's just more convenient. And yeah, better for me and for Sky.

I take Skylar out every Friday night, and it's something I look forward to all week. It's nothing crazy; we usually just split a bottle of wine over dinner, catch up and share what went on during our week.

Then we come back to the house and suffer through Maureen's goodnight routine, where she waggles her eyebrows, winks, and basically does everything short of flinging a box of condoms at us.

And then I take Skylar upstairs to bed, never wanting to stop, never wanting the night to end.

Before we drift off I make sure to turn on the monitor I still have set up for Olivia's room because I'm a worrywart, and the alarm on my phone that I always set for six in the morning.

I know we have at least half an hour then. Thirty minutes to kiss her sleepy eyes awake, to let her crawl on top of me and strip out of her tank top as I watch, to enjoy the pleasure of my body waking up in the best way possible, and to hold her close for a few minutes as the skies gradually shift from coal to gray to pale blue.

I want her here in my bed every night, want to wake up with her in my arms every single morning. *Good things come to those who wait.* That's what I keep telling myself.

"You're with me tonight. Is that all right?"

She wears a contented smile. "Better than all right." She takes her phone from her back pocket. "I'm setting the alarm extra early, though. I think Libs might spring out of bed earlier than usual tomorrow. That disastrous weekend when I babysat for him last spring...Remember that?"

Yep, I think to myself, *I remember it well*.

"Olivia was up at the crack of dawn that morning. No doubt she'll be looking to play with James bright and early tomorrow."

"I'll get up with her."

She tilts her head and takes me in. "That's the night that I knew."

"Knew what?"

"That I was crazy about you."

"I think you were dog tired and delirious."

"Nope. When I saw you holding James I was a goner."

"Same here."

"What?"

"When I came in and saw you holding him, I just…I realized how much I want that again."

"A baby?"

I swallow, raise my head to her and nod. "I want that with you someday."

She comes closer, slowly runs her fingers from my shoulder down to my wrist, and then takes me by the hand and leads me to bed.

I can touch her everywhere, kiss every inch of her skin, come inside of her bare, the way she likes it. And that's exactly what I do.

It's not happening tonight or anytime soon, and that's all right. Skylar will finish her degree, a school will scoop her up as soon as she graduates, and I have no doubt that she'll make an incredible teacher. She wants that and I want it for her.

But someday I'm going to get down on one knee and put a ring on her finger. I'll stand by her side at the altar and pledge before God that I will love her forever. Someday I want my son or daughter to grow inside of this woman I love, to feed at her breast and to be cradled in our arms.

I want to make a family with Skylar. I want it for Olivia and I want it for myself. But it's more than wanting her. I *need* Skylar in my life because she makes every moment of every day so much better.

"I love you, Sky."

I say those words so often, but tonight I say them with her hand in mine, side by side as we drift off to sleep.

* * *

A Note From Lily

Thank you for reading Skylar and Leo's love story. And if you've come to adore them the way I have, never fear, you'll be getting more of Leo, Sky and Olivia in the books that follow. The Blackbird series continues with *Ghost on the Shore*, Grace's story.

* * *

**First love, devastating loss, and the
power of second chances.**

Grace Dawson has it all. That's what everyone thinks, anyway.

She has a big shiny diamond on her finger, a job she loves, and a life filled with family and good friends. But Grace is hanging on by a thread, and it's just about ready to break.

Everyone thinks they know her. She's the town's beloved high school teacher and the blissfully happy, soon-to-be bride. But Grace has been keeping secrets, and one decision she made over a decade ago still haunts her to this day.

Shame, secrets, and the lies we tell ourselves. Grabbing hold of that second chance is hard when you can't let go of the past.